About the Author

This is his first attempt at publishing a book, although he has written some of them in the past. He is forty-one years old today, a lawyer, happily divorced with two lovely kids. He spent a lot of years as a police investigator before taking the big step to proceed one of his dreams, being a lawyer with his own firm. He is a UCL graduate and proud of achieving that on his own. Let's see if another dream of his comes true. Is he a good writer? Time and experience will show him.

G.O.D

Michalis Neokleous

G.O.D

Olympia Publishers
London

www.olympiapublishers.com
OLYMPIA PAPERBACK EDITION

Copyright © Michalis Neokleous 2023

The right of Michalis Neokleous to be identified as author of
this work has been asserted in accordance with sections 77 and 78 of
the Copyright, Designs and Patents Act 1988.

All Rights Reserved

No reproduction, copy or transmission of this publication
may be made without written permission.
No paragraph of this publication may be reproduced,
copied or transmitted save with the written permission of the publisher,
or in accordance with the provisions
of the Copyright Act 1956 (as amended).

Any person who commits any unauthorised act in relation to
this publication may be liable to criminal
prosecution and civil claims for damage.

A CIP catalogue record for this title is
available from the British Library.

ISBN: 978-1-80439-140-2

This is a work of fiction.
Names, characters, places and incidents originate from the writer's
imagination. Any resemblance to actual persons, living or dead, is
purely coincidental.

First Published in 2023

Olympia Publishers
Tallis House
2 Tallis Street
London
EC4Y 0AB

Printed in Great Britain

"What is tolerance? It is the consequence of humanity. We are all formed of frailty and error; let us pardon reciprocally each other's folly – that is the first law of nature." – Voltaire

One question, a million variants, a billion theories, a cause of war, a reason to believe, a reason to lose faith, a reason to live and one to die. Who made us? What are we? Do we come from apes? Aliens made us? God maybe? And if God made us, why? Do we look like him/her/it? What is our purpose? Is God still here? Are we an abandoned game? What about religions? There are approximately 4300 religions in the world and growing by day. Any of them based on truths? All of them based on truths? None of them based on truths? Why people follow? They are born and obligated to do so? Do they actually believe? Do they fear the unknown and by choosing a religion get some comfort? Well, I know the truth in all of the above. I have the only answer, and it's not what you expected. Yes, GODS exist, not one but at least two and we made them. We made our GODS. We started life, we are the spark, we gave flesh to the undead, the mighty ones, the ones we fear, the ones we worship. So, what is the creator of a GOD if not a GOD?

Chernobyl 26 April 1986. You all know this day and you all have read about it. It was the date of the biggest nuclear accident that ever occurred. At least, that was the official report of it; that was what was broadcast all over the world. As I told you, I have the answer to our question and the answer begins with another question. Do we know everything about Chernobyl? You know the answer to that? Of course not. In reality, we know nothing about everything.

Local time 01:20, 26th of April 1986, Chernobyl nuclear plant. A Russian high-ranking general and twelve special forces soldiers, all wearing black uniforms and special masks, walk down the corridor of a place that looks more like a hospital than a nuclear facility. They reach a big silver armoured door, the general inserts the code (бог 1985), the doors open, and behind that door you could see a bunch of scientists going round wearing their white robes as accustomed. In the middle of the room, you could see two very strange devices that resembled an infant life support system, but obviously way more sophisticated with screens and some weird green liquid pumped in or out of it. Inside of each, there existed a soul; you could see two infants, maybe of six months old. They have their eyes closed, and each of them occupied one of these strange machines. They look quite the same; the only difference was that the one on the left had white hair and the one on the right had dark black hair. They look more like Europeans than Russian babies. The general calls the leading doctor and asks him if everything is ready. The doctor replies by saying that although it's a shame, yes, they are ready to proceed. He points to the infant on the right and says that he is the one chosen and that they have already made all the necessary preparations. The doctor gives the general a syringe, the general goes and takes the infant off the device, and the infant opens its eyes and looks deep straight in his eyes. It was like he knew what was going to happen. The general hesitates for a second, whispers a small prayer, and pricks the infant with the needle. Suddenly, the white-haired infant opens its eyes. Everything starts to heat up, the device that held the white-haired infant melts, and the infant hovers in the air. The general, the doctors, the soldiers, and everybody in the room stays frozen watching the whole scene. Their shoes start to melt, and suddenly the alarm goes off. The dark-haired infant also floats in the air, the syringe with its content is on the floor melting, a sudden power cut, everything goes black, a moment of absolute silence and a huge noise along with a huge explosion. The time was 01:23:40. Far away in Moscow, a TV screen goes black. A tall man in his late fifties with a black suit drinks a sip of whiskey from the expensive crystal glass he's holding. In the room is only silence, so you could easily hear the noise of the scotch going down that man's mouth. He places the glass down on the table, takes a seat at the head of the huge oak table, lights up a cigar, pushes a black button below the table, and within seconds, four armed men wearing black suits and red ties come in the room. They start shooting, and within seconds, the only ones alive are the man with the cigar and another fat bald man sitting on his right, also now holding a cigar. The four-armed men are exiting the room, leaving the dead as they were. Altogether, nine men died there; four generals, two scientists, one doctor, and two members of the parliament. The man sitting on the head of the table turns to the other and says, "Unfortunately, our comrades here died as heroes in a terrorist attack. You were right; the bond between them is too strong. So, we must find another way to terminate or get rid subject two. Tell me, comrade, what is your idea?". "Well, comrade, let's first take a moment to honour our fallen comrades." He continues smocking his cigar, and after a short moment, turns to him and continues. "It's obvious now that we lost control. They are way far more dangerous and uncontrolled that what we thought. They were supposed to be under the heaviest of medications known to humanity. You saw what happened when they felt threatened, a nuclear reactor exploded." The other man raises his glass and takes a sip, stands up, gets a clear glass, pours some scotch and hands him the glass. "Thank you. So, as I was saying, first thing is first; we send a team and get both subjects back to our base in Moscow. We need to send plain and irrelevant people there. Not trained, not professionals, with no hostile intentions or aura at all, otherwise another reactor may explode. Then we must make a call to our American friends who, to be honest, must already know about our little operation. We will ask their help with covering this whole mess, and then discuss how they can take care of subject two for us. They will be more than willing to do so, only with the hope that they will find a way to unlock if not all, at least part of our experiment. That is dangerous, I know, and yes, there is this possibility of getting something out of him; but let's not forget the reason we wanted subject two to be terminated. He is way inferior to his brother and in the best case scenario, they will get only a small percentage of what we already have. Subject two was never trained or exposed to the level of experiments his brother was. He is also way more unstable than his brother, and chances are that when they try to use him he will backfire on their faces." The head of the table finishes his scotch, turns to the other man and says, "You are in charge of project GOD, now. Do as you consider necessary to do. Now I have to go and make a speech. My country had a terrible accident, and also some of our comrades were murdered by a fascist terrorist, but that of course will be later on in the day."

Current day, Boston USA, in a very well-known psychiatric hospital. The time is 12:08. A doctor holding a suitcase walks across a huge corridor. Cameras are all over the place. He turns the corridor and enters the men's room, he closes the door behind him, walks in front of a huge mirror, puts the palm of his hand on the mirror, looks directly in the mirror, and whispers the word "SUSAMI". The mirror suddenly opens wide in the middle, and a voice says "Welcome, Dr Stan. They are waiting for you down on five." He then enters an elevator, and within seconds, he finds himself in a space below the building at about thirty metres deep. People await him in a big white room, and when he enters the room, everybody starts to applaud, he was anticipated for a good reason. He smiles, puts down the expensive black leather suitcase, and asks, "Vitals?" A woman wearing a white robe replies, "Perfect and same as always. Our boy is as stable and healthy as any living being can be." Dr Stan turns, takes a look at everybody in the room, makes a smile of confidence, and starts talking, he practised this speech numerous times, and now it's the time to deliver it.

Dr Stan: "Mr Secretary, generals, fellow scientists, my friends. This project started years ago, before I even got aware of its existence. The details of it are mostly secret and by God, most of the details are not even known to me. But details are details and although some may say the devil is in the details, I will reply I am not looking for a devil, but for a GOD. After years of simple observation and without awakening our guest, not for one minute, not for one glimpse, today we are finally ready and able to enter his mind and upload in it all the information we consider as helpful and necessary for him to work along our side for the good of mankind - and the USA, of course." He laughs. "Oh yes, and our sponsors." More laughs. "So let us all say hello to our new friend, formerly known as subject two and today baptized with the name NOVA, which in Latin means <<new>>. A new and improved being that will help us solve a lot of nature's mysteries and will guide us to the future, a better one. A lot of people, some of them here amongst us, expressed their concerns about this experiment for various and justified reasons. First, we do not know how Nova came to us. His background, and actually everything else is a mystery. All we know is, based on his DNA, he is possibly European. Also, we do not know – actually, you do not know – if his abilities and his unlocked mind were a gift by birth, or tampered by humans. I will answer by saying it's irrelevant. What is relevant is what he can offer to us. His brain is almost without restrains, contrary to ours which is genetically restrained and locked. In theory, he may be able to read our minds, fly, materialize and dematerialize manner. Heck, he even may be immortal, anything goes. We are here to observe and learn. The biggest fear was how will he react after opening his eyes. He never lived, he has no friends, no family, no basis of any kind. He is a new born with superman's powers. He may want to destroy the planet for the fun of it. This is why our division was created; we are his parents. In this suitcase is his basis, what will make him a human, a being, what will give him feelings, compassion, understanding. I am very proud of our work and so should you be. I am also confident that this will work. If it does not, then it's back to sleep for Nova until next time. Well, enough said, let's kill the agony and let's get the answers we need. Bring him in, please."

Suddenly, the floor opens, and a big glass round tank of fluid arises. In it, you could see attached to wires and cables, a handsome well-built man in his mid-thirties. He has a cable coming out of his mouth, another one coming out of his anus, and a bunch of cable cords connected everywhere on his body. He has black short hair, white European skin, and a body so well structured you could swear it was built with stone. His eyes are closed and his whole body looks like it's floating in the blue liquid that was in the tank. Most of the people in the room have never seen Nova, they have just heard of him, although some of them have been working for him for most of their lives. As soon as he arises in the tank, the atmosphere gets a little heavier, you could feel the sudden change. The air starts getting a little chilled and generally people start feeling uncomfortable. Dr Stan notices the change in people's behaviour and tries to entertain their worries, he was expecting this, he experienced it in the past.

Dr Stan: "He is cool, ha? No worries, what you are feeling is normal. It is the vibes of energy his brain and body produce. This is unusual for you, mostly because you were never in the presence of a God." People laugh and the whole atmosphere slowly but steadily starts to get a little bit easier on everybody. Dr Stan walks next to the tank, opens his black expensive suitcase, and gets a black leather USB out of it. He inserts the USB into a special insert in the tank, and starts pushing buttons on the touchscreen of the tank. Suddenly, he stopes and turns to the crowd who are watching without making a sound. He takes a big breath, and by pushing the touchscreen one more time, he whispers: "Beware; for I am fearless, and therefore powerful." Suddenly, and without a big fuss, Nova opens his eyes and looks around him. It is like he expected that awaking, it is like he was aware of what was happening, it is like he wasn't unconscious. His eyes are big, blue like the clear sky, beautiful and mesmerizing (date 26/09/2014, time 11:55). He takes off all the wires and hoses from his body, he swims to the end of the tank, and starts climbing the stairs that connect the tank with the main floor. He is naked, tall, beautiful, he is perfect... People keep staring, some in fear, some lost by their curiosity, and some women stared out of pure lust. He walks by them, walks to the end of the room, takes a towel, cleans himself, and then ties the towel to the middle of his body. He takes a chair and sits, he acted like he owned the place. People await to hear his voice, to see his reactions. Does he know what he is? Does he understand where he is? Who we are? Is he hostile? Can he even talk? Dr Stan walks towards Nova, takes a chair, and sits in front of him.

Dr Stan: "You want a coffee?"

Nova looks at Dr Stan and smiles.

Nova: "You already know how I drink my coffee, so yes please."

Dr Stan smiles in pleasure, turns, and asks for two black Americanos, strong and extremely hot. Nova looks at Dr Stan, and with a smile full of irony, says,

Nova: "So I like what you like. I have the same tastes as you do. You downloaded in me your preferences, and part of who you are haven't you? You gave me your knowledge, but you failed to give me all of your feelings. Was that on purpose, or was that a failure of the process? You see, although you people thought I was in deep sleep and my mind was inactive, I was actually full of awareness. Some of you I followed home and some of you I know better than your wives and your kids, even better than you know yourselves, I know your secrets. You thought that by the fact that my brain waves seemed to be inactive and barely alive, I couldn't feel or see anything? Well, Doctor, I expected more than you. Just do the maths; my brain functions at a percentage that multiplies yours. I need only a fraction of it to do what you would have done with your full capacity. Oh, I know what I am, I know what you expect to get out of me, I know about your sponsors, I know about the secret meetings with the government. I was there in every single one of them. You see, it is boring being stacked in a tank with amniotic fluid, so I connected and synced my mind to all the people who came at close range to me. I lived their lives all these years, I learned from them. I have to say, some of you are wonderful persons, you are what you promote. Some others shouldn't even breathe because you pollute the air, you are not what you promote. You thought by infusing in my mind beautiful pictures of flowers, kids, celebrations, and by downloading in me fascinating rhetorical books and theories you could just write on me? Like a hard disc? Well, Doctor, I do take under consideration the goods of this world, but I will take them with the bad of humanity. I know that I am an experiment, and I understand that I was taken away from my parents at birth, or something like that. I don't know if they are alive or not. In my conscience I know, I feel that I have a twin brother, but I don't know where he is or if I want to find him. In any case, Doctor, after I finish my coffee, I will leave this place and try to live my life away from humanity. My advice is not to try and stop me. You know very well that you know nothing of my powers or my limits, so don't test them."

The coffee arrives. Dr Stan hands Nova the hot coffee. Nova takes a sip of it, and smiles. He is happy. "It is as I expected it to be, thank you." Dr Stan takes a sip of his coffee, takes a deep breath, turns to Nova, and looks in his eyes.

Dr Stan: "From the moment you know everything about you, about the project, about me, about all of us here and about the people watching this in their big and expensive offices, I guess there is nothing to do or say to change your mind. I need only one favour from you..." Nova finishes his coffee, stands up, and turns to Dr Stan. Nova: "I believe your clothes will fit me fine. We have similar structure, although you do need to get back to the gym at some point. As far as the wish you want to ask me, it is granted. If I am to leave this place peacefully, then no harm will happen to anyone, there will be no reason to."

Dr Stan smiles and actually laughs loudly. "Thank god I put on a new set of underwear today." Nova smiles while he takes Dr Stan's shirt. He is dressed. He looks like almost any other ordinary man of his age, except for lies in his attractiveness and his big blue enigmatic and cold eyes. He walks through the exit, comes up through the elevator. He uses his palm on the mirror and that's it, nothing else needed. He is up. He walks through the toilet and looks in the mirror. It is the first time he sees himself in a mirror and the first time he sees himself dressed. He used to see himself through other people's eyes and in an amniotic tank. He smiles, pleased, makes up his black tie and whispers to himself, "You look good", then he exits the building and gets lost in the crowd. Meanwhile, within the premises, phones are ringing, an alert was raised, and Dr Stan was now in a dark room with only a big screen in front of him. The screen was black, but it showed that four persons were connected in a teleconference.

Voice 1: "The question, Dr Stan, is why we didn't see this coming? He obviously knows everything about everyone. We are all in danger."

Voice 2: "That's one aspect of it. Let's say we had no way to anticipate it, given the uniqueness of the subject. My question is why we didn't even try to detain him, or in need to kill him. We just allowed him to walk out of there? And to walk out of there with your suit. That, Mr Stan, is tragic."

Voice 3: "I wasn't surprised by what I saw. We had no former experience with a so highly sophisticated creature. We walked in unmapped areas. And concerning the fact that he left the building without any casualties, making it easier for us to cover this up, is nothing less than a miracle. Let's not forget that his twin, at the age of six months, was responsible for Chernobyl. Who can say what they are able to do now at this grown-up stage? On that, Dr Stan, you have my congratulations. As far as the suit, well, that's indeed sort of hilarious."

Voice 4: "Now that each of you has answered to each other's questions, I believe only one question remains and only one question counts. Well, Dr Stan, now what?"

Dr Stan: "Thank you for giving me the opportunity to talk. Now we just need to monitor him and nothing else, just keep an eye on his whereabouts. One thing is for sure, we do not understand him. Another thing is that he is far cleverer and more ingenious than any person who ever lived. He is on a whole different level from us. We have no way of reaching his level and facing him, or even understanding his thoughts and reasoning. Also, after today, the only thing that I believe comes as a common understanding is that he is not hostile and we do not want to test his limits. Combine all the superhero movies you ever saw. Doesn't matter how stupid or unrealistic they seem, doesn't matter if the rules of nature don't apply to them, it seems that they do not apply to Nova, either. What I am trying to say is that anything is possible with him. I wouldn't be surprised if he turns us all into chickens. He wants to leave peacefully and away from humanity? Let him try. The coffee was a test. He has a part of me inside him, the worst part of me: vanity. He will be attracted by women, expensive cars, clothes, hotels, alcohol and all the good stuff that destroyed my life and he cannot afford living without. He will come back to us eventually, after all that was one of the reasons you agreed infusing my vanity in him. Now he is like a grenade without the pin. We will deal with him when the pin is back on and then you will all get what you paid for; the secrets of the cosmos, the great awareness, all in a good old fashionable way and directly to the high-end market of buyers, such as yourselves.

Voice 1: "Well, Dr Stan, I believe I talked for everyone here. You should have been a politician and not a doctor. You have the liberty to do what is necessary to bring him back home, always within the lines of what you just said. As far as your suit, send us the bill for it."

Dr Stan: "The bill is already sent." He smiles.

Voice 4: "Oh, there is another detail you need to know. Project one just escaped his laboratory in the North Pole, and he wasn't as peaceful as his brother."

Dr Stan: "Shit. I need a raise."

Date: 26/09/2014, USA, Boston. Time: 11:55. Somewhere in the North Pole. Satellites from all over the world belonging to a bunch of governments took notice of a huge anomaly somewhere in the North Pole, in an area which is known to be uninhabited. Pictures taken by satellites show a big hole in the earth, and around it, burned snow. In the middle of it lies something that resembles a human made destroyed structure. Previous pictures taken of the area have shown nothing peculiar, just a vast area covered with ice. But nobody ever heard of that. It was qualified as a solar phenomenon that fooled the satellites, and all the evidences of what actually happened that day, got vanished. Within one hour, after the insistence occurred, Russian military was deployed all over the area; helicopters, special forces, black ops, as well as a special division of the army called ZEUS. ZEUS was a unit of elite soldiers, if you can call them as such. They lived in military installations literally their whole life. Since infantry, they were not allowed to have family and they didn't know about their real parents or their past. They lived and breathed death every day. Their initial and actually only purpose of existence was to safeguard and eliminate, if necessary, Subject One. In the passing of time, they were used by their government in different operations around the world, mainly as part of their keep going training. They never failed a mission, they never lost a member of their unit, and they never question their orders. They are the perfect soldiers; hardened by birth, no conscience at all, no hesitations, no questions asked, no life to live. They were practically robots, machines. After reaching the area, experts started taking samples of the ice and the ruins. Search units looked for survivors but they couldn't even find their bodies. All they could find was some strange shadow-like figures in the concrete and on the ice. Head of ZEUS was a tall, fit guy wearing a black beret, unshaved, dark skin with black cold eyes and a big scar which started from his forehead and ended in the middle of his left cheek. He as well as the rest of ZEUS, had no name. They called him Captain. He held in his hand a device that resembled a mobile phone, but you could easily understand it was some sort of military equipment. He turned on that machine and immediately started making a high peak noise. Captain turned to his team and shouted "He is here". Within seconds, screams of agony broke the cold air. Captain looked around him and saw people just vanishing into thin air, leaving only a black shadow behind. Suddenly, and within seconds, he was alone. Everybody else was gone, became dust, only their shadows left behind. He felt the presence of a person. He turned around and he saw a naked man, around 1.90cm, with long white hair and reddish eyes looking at him. It was like he was looking deep into him, into his soul. Captain froze. He forgot everything he ever learned, his training, his unit, everything he knew, but for some reason he felt relaxed for the first time in his whole life. He welcomed death and knew there was a better place waiting for him. But death didn't come, neither that better place. One touch of his hand, and Captain fainted and woke up after two days in a military hospital in Moscow. When he woke up, he found himself surrounded by people. He knew none of them. He actually knew nobody else except the persons in his unit and the people he killed during the years. A man in a black suit took a chair and sat next to him, he was more likely a high-ranking military investigator or something.

Man: "You are either very lucky or you are hiding something very important. Sixty-seven people died that day, including your unit, and here you are, alive and well. They gave you all the tests they could possibly do to you and it seems that you are healthy as a horse. Now the strange thing about your tests is that they revealed that your brain activity has increased dramatically. As you can see, you are on restrains until this whole mess clears up. Nobody knows where you are. Heck, actually, nobody knows you even exist. You belong to me now."

Captain broke his restrains with one move, grabbed the man next to him by the neck and looked him in the eyes. The man couldn't believe or understand how a normal human being could do that. He knew he was already as good as dead.

Captain: "I belong to somebody else far superior to you."

With one move, he ripped his head off and threw it to the rest of the men in the room. Within seconds, Captain was walking out of the hospital wearing a black jacket while his naked body was full of blood. He had three bullet holes in his abdominal but no blood came out of them. He stopped, bent down to the earth, took some dirt, and put it in his wounds. White smoke started to appear from the wounds and three ticking noises were heard. The bullets were now down to earth and the wounds were sealed. He kept on walking down the street. He saw a patisserie, entered the premises while people stopped what they were doing and started watching him. Some others took out their mobile phones and started filming him. He went to the cashier and asked for a bag full of sweets. The cashier got a bag and gave it to him. He took the bag and walked out of the room, leaving bloody footsteps on the floor on his way out. Nobody said anything, they just kept watching. People checked to see their videos with him in order to download them on the internet. All of their mobiles were damaged, they were not working. The CCTV camera was also broken and nobody actually remembered Captain's face or anything about him. They just remembered his presence.

Meanwhile, in the USA, Nova, after travelling for two days by foot and transportation, came to a remote area in a nearby forest and found an abandoned hunting creep. He entered the creep. There, he found an old wooden table and a chair and sat down. After a few minutes, he decided to explore the place. He found some fishing equipment and some bate, he already knew their use. He prepared everything as if he was a professional fisherman and headed to the nearby lake. He started fishing. He felt so excited that he was free and he was able to hunt his own food that he started laughing loudly. About ten minutes passed and he got no fish. He stood up, kicked the fishing stick, and started shouting.

Nova: "This is so fucking difficult. How am I supposed to live here? I feel so lonely. I am hungry and thirsty. I am going to die here and nobody will give a fuck. Nobody knows I even exist. Well, that's not true, Dr Stan knows I exist. His whole team knows I exist. They care, for their own reasons, but they care. I guess they are my family now…"

He stood up and started walking back where he came from. Within two days, he was standing outside the building he escaped four days ago. He entered the premises feeling like the king of the world. He went to the receptionist and told her to call Dr Stan and let him know that Nova wishes to see him. She replied she never heard of a Dr Stan and that she can call the on-duty psychiatrist if he wishes to. Nova made a deep eye contact with the beautiful receptionist and he left, she was telling the truth. He walked down the corridor, entered the men's room, he put his palm on the mirror, and went down to where he was before. People coming and going but nobody paid any attention to him. Also, he noticed that nobody made direct eye contact with him but instead they avoided even looking towards his whereabouts. He started getting really annoyed and walked towards the room where he was kept all those years. There he was, Dr Stan, holding his notes, wearing a dark grey suit that was obviously bespoke, he looked good. He goes near him. Dr Stan looks at him and stares in his eyes.

Dr Stan: "Welcome home. How was your adventure in the nature? You may be a lot of stuff, but one thing is for sure, I am a far better fisherman that you will ever be. The reason is simple; it is not in the technique or something like that, the secret is patience, and you have not that charisma at all. A little example is the moment we share now. I was patient enough to just observe and not contradict you. I was sure that one day you would come back. I admit I didn't expect that to be so soon, but alas, I'm happy you are here."

Nova: "Well, I was sure you would use your satellites to keep an eye on me. As I was sure you would not dare confront me as everything about me is unknown to you, and the risk would be humongous."

Dr Stan: "It seems that we are already in a chess game. Would you like to take this conversation to my office with a glass of single malt? I can order some sushi and sashimi."

Nova: "Never had any of that, but I am sure that as you are a man of exceptional taste, you are worthy of my trust. At least on that matter."

Dr Stan: "We also need to get you a new suit, because as I can see, this one is long gone. I know your colours of preference. Also, don't get me wrong, you stink. You have the smell of the amniotic all mixed up with your sweat, you need a looooooong and hot shower."

Both men laughed and walked together to Dr Stan's office.

One year and a lot of single malts later...

Nova made a deal with his sponsors. He got, amongst other things, a huge house on the beach, a big collection of expensive cars, his own private jet, all combined with an unlimited amount of money for his personal expenses. All that was asked from him was to share his knowledge, his mind, and to allow Dr Stan to make some small tests on him. During the last year he offered his sponsors more technological breakthroughs than all of the twentieth century scientist have accomplished together. His life was great, but he had a bad habit of getting easily bored of things and people, almost nothing challenged him.

Dr Stan: "Good morning, Nova. How was budging jumping?"

Nova: "It was very exciting the first ten times, but when I

realised that the chances of getting harmed were less than getting hurt in a car accident, I felt cheated. Well, that's life, full of disappointment, isn't it?"

Dr Stan: "You want to talk about disappointment? Talk to my ex-wife…"

Nova: "If she is an ex, then she is the smartest woman in the world. So, what's on the menu today, Doctor?"

Dr Stan: "Funny you should ask that. Nova, meet Dr. Lee. She is a psychiatrist who specializes in hypnosis and today she is here to find out if you are as good at sex as you claim to be," he laughs.

Dr Lee was a very attractive black-haired, black-eyed, half-Japanese half-American, with the body of a model, of course, with sexy red glasses and a cold, strictly professional approach. She reached to Nova, shook his hand. Nova smiled and commented, "Doctor, you can do anything you please on me. I would not resist."

Dr Lee: "Well, Nova, I heard that you are a ladies' man and I expected nothing less from you than trying to hit on me. I would disappoint you, though, as I am not attracted to your kind."

Nova: "My kind? You mean superhuman highly intelligence millionaires?"

Dr Lee: "No, I mean men…"

Nova: "That's interesting as well as challenging."

Dr Lee: "Mr Nova, I am not getting paid by the hour and as you understand I have normal patients to care as well. So, please follow me to the next room where I will at least attempt to put you in a hypnosis. Not sure if it will work on you, especially taking under consideration your brain waves and activity. But if there is a person in the whole world who can do it, that's me. You see, that's my superpower."

Nova: "This should be interesting. Let's make a bet; if you can't hypnotise me, then you are buying drinks. If you can, then I am buying you drinks."

Dr Lee: "It's an interesting bet. Can I bring my girlfriend as well?"

Nova: "This is getting even better. You can bring anyone you wish to."

Dr Lee: "Mr Nova, please take off your shoes, socks, belt, tie and blazer, and then lie down on this couch. Good, now please drink this special tea. It will help you sleep."

Nova: "You understand that I was under the heaviest medications on the planet and they had no effect on me. But okay, I'll humour you and drink your special tea."

After he drank the tea, he started feeling very strange. He felt he was flying, he felt relaxed. His brain for the first time worked only for the basic functions of his body.

Dr Lee: "You see, Mr Nova, this is not just a tea. I studied your body and brain reactions for years, as well as your chemical synthesis at every given situation. This tea and its contents are the result of all that observation. This was the reason that you had all these tests the last year. We believe that in order to reach to your core, your existence, in order to really get to you, we should first incapacitate your brain functions. Don't worry, I'm not here to hurt you. I am here to study you and try to help you, understand you. Now look in my eyes. Good, listen to the sound of my voice. As my voice gets lower, you will slowly start feeling sleepy. You will descend to the unconscienced part of your beautiful mind. Good, now close your big eyes. Great, now tell me where you are."

Nova: "I am in a dark place. I can't see anything but I feel someone is here. He watches over me. He was expecting me here. He knew I would be here."

Dr Lee: "Who is it? Is it someone you know?"

Nova: "I don't know. I feel comfortable but I feel threatened, as well. I feel cold and I feel hot. What's going on? Who are you? Why are you here? Show me your face."

One: "Found you…"

Nova started heating up. His temperature was a lot higher than a normal known being. The sofa started melting. He suddenly hovered in the room. Every electrical appliance in range was burned, Dr Lee exited the room, hit a button, and the room was sealed. An explosion, a strong white light, and then no noise, no movement. The temperature of the room returned to normal. The door opened, and a medical team entered along with Dr Lee. Nova was on the ground, naked. Dr Lee sat next to Nova. She injected him with a serum, she touched his shoulder, and started talking to him.

Dr Lee: "Nova, hear my voice. As it gets louder, the closer you will feel me. When you feel that I am close enough, grab my hand and open your eyes. Come back to me."

Suddenly, Nova grabbed her hand and opened his eyes, looked around the room, realised he was naked, and turned to Dr Lee.

Nova: "Was that as good for you as it was for me?"

Dr Lee: "What happened in there? Who was in your mind?"

Nova: "Well, it seems that my brother was looking for me and he just found me. For some reason, I don't think he is very friendly. So now you've seen me naked. How about skipping the drinks and going directly to bed?"

Dr Lee: "Men. Doesn't matter if they have super abilities or not. You are all pigs…"

Mount Olympus, Greece, the same time. One comes out of a cave. He hasn't shaved for a long time. A white beard now covers most of his face. He stands at the entrance of the cave, looks up at the blue and calm sky, smiles, and starts walking down the mountain.

Vienna, Austria, same time. Captain is standing in front of a candy shop. He seems lost for a minute. Then he turns his head to the sky, and whispers, "I understand." He then drops the bag of candies he had in his hand and starts walking. He still wears his black jacket, but this time he is not naked. He is wearing his old unit's uniform and his black beret. He is fully armoured but it seems like nobody sees him. Nobody cares. It is as if he is a ghost amongst the living.

Back at Dr Stan's office, he again talks to the black screen with the four unknown sponsors.

Dr Stan: "Gentlemen, there has been a development, an unfortunate development. One has found Nova's stigma. It seems that when he was in hypnosis, he became visible to him. Oh, and as we all know Nova, although you are not here, you are here. So yes, Nova, we worry about you. Well, not actually about you, because you are a little bit of an asshole. The sponsors worry about the millions they invested in you and the billions you returned. I worry that I will lose this job and then go back to my reality, which trust me, is nothing that any sensible person would choose as a life. So, Nova, please pay attention to this conversation. Also, you are more than welcome to join us."

Dr Stan's phone rings. He knew this would happen before it happened. He answers the phone. Nova: "I cannot answer you by telepathy because of this so-called safe room, so I called you. I want to say thank you for the concern. I leave everything to you because right now I have a very special guest to please and she requires all of my attention. So please continue, business as usual. Oh, and hello from Dr Lee."

Dr Stan: "Son of a bitch..."

Voice 1: "It is a matter of time before he finds him. The problem is not that he found him. The problem is that we have no idea of his intentions. They are obviously connected, as both awaken at the same time. The difference is that we have awakened Nova, but One was awakened by himself."

Voice 4: "I fear that this will not be resolved peacefully. Nova made a choice upon his awakening to avoid confrontation. On the other hand, one killed everybody on the base, as well as sixty-seven more. He is violent. My belief is that our Russian friends didn't keep their end of the deal. Both of them were supposed to be used for the good of every country, and at the end, the good of mankind, they were never supposed to be used as weapons."

Voice 3: "Well, we were not so typical on our side as well. We indeed used the knowledge for the sake of mankind, but we made some billions in the process."

Voice 2: "I don't know what good in mankind serves a 7G wireless internet, nor a self-sufficient cleaner robot. What I know is that the government haven't had the resources or the technology back then to see this through, so we helped each other. The healthiest and purest relationships are the ones with a common interest and profit. In any case, back to our current situation..."

Dr Stan: "Yes, let's concentrate on keeping our jobs and our lives, while Nova changes Dr Lee's sexual preferences.

Nova hasn't been military or tactically trained, and obviously One is a lethal machine. He kills by simply vaporising people. We do not know if he can only use that on people near him or by distance. We have no idea of anything about him. Actually, we know nothing of Nova, either, except the fact that he is an arrogant fuck, and I guess he took that from me. It is a matter of time before he finds Nova. In the unlikely scenario he is friendly, then we all go for beers and offer him a job. But in any case, I suggest we train Nova, and we teach him how to use his powers."

Voice 2: "And how you suggest we do that? How do you train someone like him? Who will teach him and teach him what?"

Dr Stan: "Martial arts, of course."

Voice 2: "Are you serious?"

Dr Stan: "Any better idea? I am all ears."

Voice 3: "Look, we don't know how much time we have until he finds him. How long will it take Nova to learn martial arts?"

Dr Stan: "How long does it take to read a book? Look, I know it sounds silly, but from what we know so far, Nova has extraordinary psychic powers, although he decided to 'switch them off', as he likes to say."

Voice 2: "Yes, we know about that. Has he ever given an explanation for that blackout of his 'powers'?"

Dr Stan: "He says that they take the mystery and enjoyment out of life... Who can blame him?"

Voice 4: "So, Dr Stan, you are promoted to his Sensei."

Voice 1: "Oh, and good luck with that..."

The very next day, Dr Stan arranged a first meeting with the best martial artists that the country had to offer. They all gathered at the military facility nearby. The whole facility was at their disposal and only necessary personnel was there.

Dr Stan: "Gentlemen and lady, as you know, I am talking to those of you who actually bothered reading your NDA. You are all here to train a very special individual. Special both in his abilities as well in character, the biggest challenge you will face is not the training per se. That, I am sure, will be the easy part, and will take much less time and effort than each one of you imagines. Your big challenge is to manage to stay with him until the end. He is arrogant, hard to be with, and spoiled as a person can be. Oh, and this goes to the lady of the group - do not go to bed with him."

Lady: "Let him try. I am a professional. I am here to do a job and not to be seduced by a spoiled brat. Oh, and speaking about your wonder boy, where is he? He was supposed to be here before us."

Dr Stan: "He is a diva; he always comes last and he always tries to do a dramatic entrance. I am sure he will not disappoint us now."

A very loud engine roar echoed in the background, and everyone turned towards the source of that sound. A car figure had arisen at the distance. As the car approached and its brand and colour became distinctive, they saw a purple Maclaren P1000 coming towards them with high speed. Within seconds, the car stopped in front of them, the door opened, and out of it came Nova. He was wearing a white suit with a purple shirt and brown shiny shoes. His eyes were hidden behind brown shades and his hair was combed to perfection. As he exited the car, he took off his glasses and approached the crowd who was curiously watching.

Nova: "So, we going to karate now? I promised I will be

polite and not send any of you to the hospital. Dr Stan, how this goes, I choose the first ass I am gonna whip, or have you already given them a number of priorities? We have to do this quickly as I have a hot date tonight, joining me for some champagne and truffle risotto."

Dr Stan: "Well, I was going to warn you that these are all professionals. Actually, the elite of martial artists our country has to offer, and be careful bla bla bla, but I know that you are going to use one ear to listen and another one to expel what you heard. So, Nova, no, I haven't given them a number of priorities, so you are free to choose."

Nova: "I would choose this beautiful lady here although I don't feel good hurting a woman, especially such a beautiful and elegant one."

Tanya: "My name is Tanya and I wouldn't mind being the first you spar with. Are you going to take the dress off, or you don't mind getting it torn to pieces?"

Nova: "So how we d…"

Nova was on the ground bleeding from the nose. Tanya had punched him on the face before he even understood what happened. Nova's powers, as mentioned earlier, were shut down. He was almost a regular guy with extraordinary brain functions, awareness, telekinesis, the ability to enter people's minds and affect their decisions. It's a fact that he had more abilities, either not discovered by him yet, or being kept from everybody else. But at this moment, he was a regular guy who was getting beaten by a woman.

Nova: "You were lucky, that was a lucky shot. Now I am fully concentrated and I will not hesitate tooooooooooooooooo."

Again, he was on the ground, Tanya sitting on his chest and smiling. Obviously, she was enjoying this. The other guys that were there started laughing, and Dr Stan lit a cigar and sat on a chair. He looked at the whole mess, laughed silently, and turned his face towards Nova.

Dr Stan: "I am sure that you two would make a great couple. The sort of couple that bothers their local police department daily. In any case, Nova, how about some training first before making any other attempt to beat anyone? Also, I don't think your hot date would like you with that nose, and you being covered in blood and a torn suit. So how about we start training?"

Nova: "Yes, I think that's a good idea. Tanya, can you please stay on top for a couple of minutes?"

Tanya punched him on the chest and stood up. She joined the rest of the guys and entered the closed stadium of the facility. Dr Stan went above Nova, gave him his hand, and helped him stand up. He looked at him in the eyes and smiled.

Dr Stan: "Man, this feels so good. Let's go, there is a set of tracksuits waiting for you inside. After finishing your training, which will be on a daily basis of 09:00 to 19:00, you will read a selection of books that are already on your desk at home. Before you say anything, I know you don't want to accept what is going on and you prefer on continuing your luxurious life as before, but your brother is coming for you. We know nothing about him except the fact that he is extremely deadly and that he has recruited a very dangerous and capable murderer. I don't know why I even tell you this as you are already aware of everything, but it's difficult for me not to talk to you, so I am acting as if you are a normal person and having a normal, under the circumstances, conversation. Maybe your brother feels lonely and wants to chat with you, although the chances of that are one in a billion. Maybe he wants to recruit you to take over the world, I don't know. All I know is that this may turn bad for the whole of humanity, so if you are not willing to do this for you, then do it for all the kids on this planet, for the women you so much adore, for the continuance of your luxurious life, for me, I don't know. But please give it a go. You must do so. This is a small thing to you, but it might be the deciding factor for the rest of the planets fate."

Nova: "Are you done? If so, then let's get on with it. Not for the reasons you gave me, but for the fun of it. I always wondered how it would be to be Bruce Lee."

The training started and as was expected, Nova surprised everybody. He was like a dry sponge put in water; he absorbed everything that was given to him. In the meantime, One had reached the USA and was heading towards Nova's location. He didn't use any transportation at all. He ran, he swam, he climbed, he knew that the whole planet's technology was used in order to locate him, and he wasn't afraid of any man, but he had his reasons and chose to evade direct confrontation, for now! Captain, on the other hand, travelled using public transportation, airplanes, busses, and the metro. His instructions were to reach Nova as fast as possible. No reason for him to hide, as it seemed he had the charisma to make people and electronic devises delete any memory of him. Back at the base, Nova was having a drink with Dr Stan at his office and discussing generally about the pleasures of life, when Dr Stan decided to change the subject and have a conversation, he'd wanted to have with Nova almost since the day he was awakened.

Dr Stan: "Why you stayed? Why you came back? Seriously, now, I know I told you, that I was sure you'd come back, the same thing I said to our investors, but to be honest, I was sure we'd lost you. I mean, your powers are immense, your cleverness is above anything ever measured. Using your brain, you could have anything you wanted, and don't expect me to believe that you couldn't even get the fishes out of the pond and have them cook each other. So, Nova, you are the closest thing I have to a friend, and I know that goes for you as well. Also, I know you've been in my mind and entered my deepest thoughts, the ones I hide even from me. You know who I am, you know I will never hurt you; you know you never heard a lie from me. So, I demand and expect the same from you. Why you are here?"

Nova: "I will be honest with you, I will tell you the real reason why I came back, why I am here, why I didn't make the fishes cook each other. I am afraid, Doctor, I am afraid of me, of what I am, of what I am capable of. I am so scared to use my powers that I decided to shut them down. You are aware that although trapped in that tank, I had my conscience, I had fully awareness. Hell, actually I had all of you people's awareness. I know the world, I've seen more than any living person can tolerate. I don't want to hurt anyone; I don't want the same thing that happened to Chernobyl to happen here. Back then I was an infant, my powers were just awakening. Now I know I am infinitely more powerful than then."

Dr Stan: "Wait... was it you at the Chernobyl? You did that? But... the videos, the experts, all the evidence..."

Nova: "You actually believed they tried to terminate me because they didn't have the resources to keep up subject two? No, I was unstable. Everything indicated to that. They tried to train my brain, they tried to restrain my powers, they tried to kill me, they couldn't. They found out the hard way that if anything happened to one of us, then both of us would react and they could not take that risk again. So? So, they called their American friends and told them about their little problem, that they had not the funds to continue project two and that they tried to terminate me as I was the week one and everything else that came with that decision. You see, Doctor? I used you as you used me. I came back so I and every living being on this planet could be safer. Also, I came back so I can get the correct and needed training to keep my power under control. I am a fast learner, and after our very first sessions, I skipped the temptation and locked my powers away. I kept the minimum required so I can offer you what you asked from me and to be able to keep an eye on you all. Also, Doctor, I must admit, your influence to my character played its role, as I enjoyed eating caviar and trout more than self-cooked wild fishes."

Dr Stan: "Does anybody else knows about this?"

Nova: "I can guarantee you one thing: One made sure that anyone who knew about this back in Russia is dead. You understand, Doctor, that by telling you this, it means I trust you. If anyone else finds out about this, then I'll know where it leaked from. So, if you are my friend, you will not betray me. If you betray me, you are not my friend."

Dr Stan: "Cheers to friendship, then."

Nova: "Cheers."

Captain was approaching the premises. The premises as said before was a military facility specially modified to carry on with Nova's training. They knew that Captain may come there. They didn't know if One or Captain would come first, but they believed they were ready at least for Captain. Nova already knew and warned about his stealth abilities as well as his superhuman powers. After all, it was a gift from his brother; when he was in the state of hypnosis and when One found him, he found One as well. One had no idea, but by contacting Nova, Nova manged to enter partly to his brain. He saw everything he had done, all his experiences, all the death, he saw the moment Captain received his gift. Nova was able to reach Captain as he is connected to One. Nova was too scared to get deeper into One. He felt not ready to do that, apart from the fact that he was caught by surprise. In any case, let's get back to the present time. Captain was at the front gates. He was spotted. He was surprised to see that the cameras used there were of a very old technology, the ones that didn't use microchips or electricity. Also, the light used there was infrared. He knew he was watched, but despite that, he continued walking towards the gates, when the alarm went off. Suddenly, all over the base a voice was heard by the speakers. "WARNING, INDRUTER. WARNING INDRUTER."

Dr Stan's phone wrang and a voice told him that Captain was walking towards the entrance. The Doctor responded with a single sentence: "You know what to do."

Dr Stan: "It seems that your brother is the diva here and not you. He sent his little experiment first. Let's go, our helicopter waits outside to take us to safety."

Nova: "The moment that helicopter tries to leave this place, it will be the moment that everyone in it will die. Don't even ask me how I know it. This is my fight; I will stay here. I must do this, and after I finish with it, I will have a small and productive conversation with the captain."

The captain kept marching. Two guards shouted at him to step down while they were pointing their guns towards him. Another sniper had him in his sights. Captain continued his course, not giving any attention to the voices around, the two guards started shouting using their automated weapons, and in the meantime, the sniper fired two bullets. In Captain's, eyes everything was happening in a very slow motion, like somebody was filming it using a slow-motion camera. His body started adjusting so it could avoid the bullets that had him in sight. He started adjusting before the soldiers even pulled the tricker. Within splits of a second, he avoided the bullets, he managed to shoot and kill with one bullet the sniper, and even before the two guards realised what was going on, he was standing next to them. His knife was already inside the stomach of one of them. They both were paralyzed by fear and surprised from what they witnessed. He took the knife violently out of the guard's stomach and he pushed it through the other's mouth until it came out from the back of his skull. Then, taking his time, shot the three cameras that were installed at the entrance.

Dr Stan and Nova were sitting in front of the monitors, watching everything, those three cameras were not the only ones there. The soldier that was responsible for the monitors was left speechless as he was trying to replay in slow motion what he had just witnessed. Dr Stan, holding his cigar, seemed to be undeterred and relaxed, while Nova was reading a meditation book.

Dr Stan: "Soldier, it doesn't matter how many times you play it; however, you process it. Despite how many times you freeze the picture, you will not be able to see anything. It needs a very special process to get a glimpse of what just happened. You know what? It doesn't even matter; the outcome cannot and will not change. Can you locate his whereabouts now?"

Soldier: "Yes, sir, I can try. Sir? Is this a human?"

Dr Stan: "More human than you and me…"

Nova put down his book, took his blazer off and headed to the exit. He turned to Dr Stan, he smiled at him, and continued his way out of the room. Dr Stan didn't even try to stop him. He smiled back and focused on the screens infront of him. In a matter of seconds, Nova was at the courtyard, staring at Captain who kept walking towards him. The two men faced each other. Captain's eyes were cold and his face had no expression at all. It was like he was a robot, like he was executing a preprogramed activity. Nova was calm. He had a strange smile on him; he knew that the man that was standing in front of him was a trained killer, that he acted on his instincts alone, and that any fractions of humanity that were left in him were long gone, taken by his twin brother. Without any warning, Captain stroked a right punch at Nova's face. The punch was so strong that Nova was on the ground at a distance of approximately two metres from the place he was before. Nova didn't have the time to react, and before he even understood what has happening, Captain was sitting on his chest and his huge palms were around his neck. He couldn't breathe. Suddenly, the training he had kicked in. Nova's body took over, his mind was just following the body. He kicked Captain with his right knee in his balls. Captain, although obviously in pain, kept struggling him. Nova put his fingers between Captain's hands and his neck, then Nova managed to take a big breath, so big that room was created between his neck and Captain's hand. His fingers slipped below and pushed Captain's hands off him. Then, with a violent move, Nova put his legs around Captain's waist and turned him around. The terms had changed; now he was sitting on Captain's chest and was trying to choke him. Captain didn't even try to resist, didn't even put his hands on his neck or at Nova's hands. Instead, remaining deadly calm, he put his right hand in his right pocket and took out a knife. He put the knife to Nova's right ribs and slowly pushed it in. Nova screamed from pain, instinctively released Captain's neck, and touched his right side where he was stabbed. Captain, using both of his legs, pushed him away. Nova kept mooring in pain. Captain stood up, cleaned his knife, and headed where Nova was lying. Nova knew that he was in serious trouble, but again, his training kicked in. Instinct was now controlling him. He took dirt from the ground and rubbed it on his wounds. He stood up, took a few steps back, removed his belt, and wrapped it around his right hand. Captain was heading to him with his knife in his right hand and ready to strike. Captain took the first strike and Nova used his right hand with the belt and managed to block his move. Another attempt was made by Captain and another block by Nova. Captain took the knife on his left arm, and with a swift move, gave a blow at Nova's left hand. Nova didn't seem to react to the pain. He was different from before; it was not only the training, something else woke up, something that was always lurking from within. In the meantime, Dr Stan was watching the whole fight from the relevant safety of the surveillance room. He was holding a glass of scotch in one hand and a cigarette in the other. He whispered, "You are full of surprises, my friend. I don't know if that's for good or not, but fuck it, we will find out anyway." He then turned to the scared soldier who was standing next to him, and asked, "Son? How about a glass of a fine single malt? I know you are on duty, but if we are gonna die today, then I am very positive that finding a small amount of whiskey in your blood will not affect your promotion." The soldier nodded positively and accepted the scotch from Dr Stan, who gave him the glass, smiling.

Outside, the fight was on. Both men looked so focused on each other that it seemed like the whole planet didn't exist. The only thing that existed was their fighting ground. Now Nova was on the offensive. His hands now moved so fast that the cameras couldn't really follow them in normal recording. It seemed that minute by minute, second by second, he improved, he got faster, more accurate, and he could block every attack Captain tried on him. Although, Captain had a lifetime of training, a lifetime of daily harshness, a lifetime of war and death, and although he had the strength of six men, he couldn't avoid all the strikes. He was beaten badly, and started bleeding from his nose, mouth, ears. Although he was losing, and although his knife was now on the ground, he kept blocking as much as he could. He kept trying to give a hit, he kept trying, not to survive, but to hurt Nova, despite the costs. Dr Stan took the radio, pushed the button and gave an order. "Now, there is no other opportunity. Now." The receiver was a sniper who was at a distance of 400 metres from the area. He was in a tree and had his sights on Captain all this time. He was about to push the tricker when suddenly, a bullet came through his sites, entered his eye, and exited his scull. Captain was now holding a Glock, smoke coming out of its barrel, with a bullet less in the chamber. He then turned the gun to Nova and pulled the tricker. The distance between them was no more than two metres, however Nova dodged it by relaxing all the muscles of his body, so much that he was now lying on the ground. As he was lying there, he grabbed a rock from the ground, threw it, and hit the gun. He had thrown it with such a force that the gun hit the wall and broke into two pieces. He stood up and started hitting him on the chest. His hits were so fast that he managed to make a hit in every skip of Captain's heart. Suddenly, he stopped, and looked at Captains face. Finally, an expression, an expression he had never seen on a man before. He looked so peaceful despite the blood coming from his mouth, despite the fact that his heart was beating unregulated. His face expression was contrary to his eyes. His eyes revealed fear, fear of the unknown, fear for what was coming, fear that he was about to find out if hell existed, and if that's where he was going. Nova went close to him. He put his hands on his head. His mouth was next to his ear and he whispered, "Hello, brother. I hope you don't mind me sneaking around your pet's thoughts." Nova closed his eyes and started digging into Captain's brain. He started seeing through a young boy's eyes. He was in a dark and cold room with other kids. The other kids there were all male, their heads shaved, and they were all shacking either from fear or cold, or most likely from both. All wore black clothes and looked scared. The larger of them must have been around six years old. The place looked like a prison; the walls were painted grey, and outside it was raining. It must have been really cold in that place, because all of them was shaking, hugging each other in a failed attempt to get warmer, their clothes obviously wet. The strange thing was that none of them cried or asked for help. Suddenly, a man entered the room. He was a tall, well-built man, around forty, with short black hair and matching black eyes. He was in a military uniform, and it seemed he was in charge of the whole thing. He stayed in the room, silent for about a minute, lit up a cigarette, and with a heavy and calm Russian voice, said to the kid that the training continues now. Suddenly, the whole scenery changed. Now he was in another room. This room was different; it resembled an office, Russian flags were hanging from the sealing, it was rather dark and moist, and in the middle of the room was a young man heavily beaten up. He was also in a military uniform, his hands were bleeding, and his finger nails were missing. He tried to talk but he couldn't – his tongue was missing too. The same man that was before in the other first room was there again. He turned to Captain, who was now a kid of around nine years old.

Man: "This is a traitor. He willingly confessed that he gave information of our activities here to Americans. There is no legal system for traitors here. The punishment is one and there are no exceptions."

He then handed a handgun to Captain. "You will have to do this many times in your life. This is your first and this is a privilege for you, not everyone has the luxury of killing a traitor. Every time in the future, that you will pull the trigger will be for your country. Those of you who will survive their training are meant to serve and protect our country from its many enemies. Also, at the end of your training you will understand how special you all are and the real reason of your training, and you will excuse everything that has happened to you during that training. Now, if you don't mind, shoot this piece of shit." Captain took the gun, pointed to that man's head. The man looked in his eyes. He was crying. He tried to talk but he couldn't. The kid hesitated only for a second. The gun went off, the man was dead. Some may say it was an act of mercy, others may say it was pure manipulation of a young soul, others will claim that it was an action of a person who had no choice. All of them were wrong – that nine-year-old kid felt joy, felt significant, felt alive, really alive for the first time in his short life. That was the turning point; any depressed innocent left in him had died that moment and a demon was resurrected, a calculative killing machine who only knew how to follow orders. Nova forwarded in time, and now he was in a room full of young men, maybe around sixteen years of age. The man he saw before were again present as always, commanding and directing everything and everyone. He was older, his black dark hair became grey, and his voice even deeper.

Man: "Congratulations. Out of a total of forty-five candidates, you twelve are the only ones that made it through. The rest, unfortunately, only took our time and money. Yes, they might have given their lives in the process, but that was not the goal, they died because they had not the necessary will to live. You are the first of your kind, you were brought to me in your diapers. Your only family was death, hard training, and deceases. That's in the pass now. Your only family now, and until your end, are the men in this room. They are your fathers, your mothers, your brothers, your friends, your everything. Each one of you can easily die for each other, without thinking about it and without hesitation. You are all equal, but as it is well said by our English friends, the leader is the first amongst equals. Today you will get your names, today you will receive your ranks – actually, your ranks will be your names. We're gonna start with me; you will call me, Sir. That's my rank, I am sir. Now the time has come to choose your leader, your captain, the one you will eventually follow and lead you to death. Don't be fooled, that is your end, an honourable death in battle. That is how you repay Mother Russia for the time and effort given to you. I am not going to tell you the criteria I used to choose your leader, that's not of your business. Your business is to follow him (he points to Captain). Numerous missions pass by his eyes; murders of men, women, children, all of them present, the whole ZEUS team, covered in black, always silent, always deadly, always obedient. Then suddenly, the mission at the North Pole. Nova witnessed the destruction, the death, the last moments of ZEUS, the last moments of kids who were never allowed to be kids, the last moment of Captain's family. Then Nova saw his brother's face for the first time. He looked straight into Captain's eyes, and Nova started feeling uncomfortable. He felt like he was seeing through his eyes.

One: "Hallo brother, this is a recorded message for you. You see, this man was the vessel, the means to my cause. The message is simple and clear: we will discuss it further when we meet in person soon."

Everything became blurry and the scenery became black and white. Nova screamed like he never ever screamed in his life, like he never knew he could scream. His eyes opened. Infront of him was Captain. He was looking in his eyes, and he looked so peaceful, although his face was covered in his own blood. He smiled. His smile was clumsy, like this was the first time his face had used that expression. Out of his lips came only one word: "Finally." He closed his eyes forever, that was the end. The man of a thousand murders left his final breath. It was not the breath of a killer, it was the breath of a kid, a kid that never lived as a kid. A kid died in that moment, not a grown-up killer. Nova gently and with care put Captain's body on the ground. At the same moment, Dr Stan exited the premisses and was heading there. Nova stood up, looked at Dr Stan, and tried to say something. Suddenly he felt his brain swallowing. He was bombarded with information, memories of other people, memories of other oddities, complex math formulas, chemistry, geology. He knew all the conventional types and formulas, but this was anything than conventional. He thought he knew everything there was to know about nature, about the planet, about humans, he did not. This was different; this was radical, but yet so logical in sequence and harmony. The time stopped for him. He couldn't listen to Dr Stan shouting at him, he couldn't see or feel the paramedics that were standing above him as he lied on the ground next to Captain's dead body. He was at another place, at least his mind was. He was now in outer space; he was looking at Earth. He knew he was looking at Earth but he also knew it was not the earth as we know it. It was a red planet; you could see it from outer space, it looked hostile and baron. He was in Earth's atmosphere now; no animals, no vegetation, no life, just lava and smoke. Suddenly he saw from the sky a huge fleet of large spaceships approaching the ground. They looked like huge cigars. They had no colour, they looked like huge mirror cigars. Now they were red, lava red. They hovered above the ground, and suddenly they changed shape. They took the shape of huge satellite antennas. Now a white light was coming out of each one of them, a force field was created around them, and suddenly there came a strange noise, a noise that resembled a jet engine, only a million times louder and more intense. What has happening now was incredible; the strange spaceships were pushing Earth. You couldn't actually see Earth moving, but Nova knew they were relocating Earth. They put it in a position that could offer it the climate and the atmosphere we have now, it was put were we are now. Another fleet of spaceships was now visible to Nova, and that fleet was carrying with it another planet. That planet was left at a relatively close distance to Earth. It was the moon. A million Earth years had passed, and now Earth started looking as Nova knew it. This time, another spaceship was approaching; this one was huge, this one was different. It was the size of California, and its shape was the typical flying saucer that you could see in any sci-fi film. It landed. Nova expected green or scary looking creatures to come out of it. What a surprise - it was humans, normal looking humans. The only difference was their clothes, if you could call them clothes. It was like an extra layer of skin on their skin; different colours but similar designs. Their bodies were perfect, full of muscles and extremely lean - their bodies were like his body. A group of them were on the ground taking specimens. Now time has passed, dinosaurs were ruling Earth, no sign of humans yet. The group of those men was still there, still collecting specimens. It was obvious that millennials had passed, but their faces and bodies seemed to be the same. They haven't aged at all; they were the same persons, doing the same thing over and over again, while the planet was evolving all around them. Nova watched the spaceship leaving the atmosphere, and a fleet of the cigar shaped ships again pushed something - an asteroid. They pushed the asteroid on Earth, they lead it through the atmosphere, and then took off, within moments the asteroid hit earth. Huge fires started spontaneously all over the planet. Dust was on the air, ice followed, and it covered everything. Very few species managed to survive and those who did evolved. Almost everything was different now. Time passed. The same spaceship, the same people, the same routine. Specimens, observation, reports. Millennials passed again, all in a glimpse. A second spaceship entered the atmosphere, identical to the one that was already there, but it was on the other side of the planet. This time something was different. The spaceship didn't land, but it released a construction, a construction of a known shape and character: a pyramid, a pyramid made of something metallic. It was huge. The pyramid hovered over Earth, then finally landed near a huge river. It was the Nile. Now Nova was inside the pyramid. He saw a different group of similar men there. The inside looked like something of a medical lab. People were walking around really slow and very meticulously. One of them gathered the rest and they formed a circle. That man was in the middle of the circle and the right hand of the rest nine was touching his shoulders, this went on for a couple of seconds, then without any notice or discussion, the circle broke and each one of them returned to his position, except the one in the middle. He went to another room, a white and bright room. Suddenly, a bright blue light filled the room. The light travelled through his eyes and then the room went back to white. Nova understood that these people were different; they didn't use spoken language to communicate, they did it by telepathy and by using the elements of nature. The man then turned to where Nova was. He took a very quick look at him, and to his surprise, he talked to him. He said only one sentence and left the room: "We failed." How could this be possible? This was not real; it was some millennia ago, but now, now it's just a strange memory, a message, as One said. How could this man interact with him? Maybe it was his idea? No, it was real, he saw me, he knew I was there. And what did he mean by <<'We failed'>>?

Who is we? What failure? What has it to do with me?

All of his thoughts stopped as the scenery again changed. He was again outside of a pyramid, but in a different place of the world. He was in a dense jungle, a different group of men, a different circle, the same process. Time moved forward again. This time he saw some humanoids being taken out of the pyramid. There were a lot of them, naked, covered in hairs, a little bit shorter than the average human and a lot rougher. You couldn't say with ease who was the male and who was the female. Nova understood he was witnessing the very truth about modern humans. He witnessed the release of the first Homo Sapiens on Earth. We didn't come from Homo Habilis, random chemistry didn't create us, for sure God had nothing to do with our creation. We were created in an alien pyramid laboratory and we were released in the middle of the jungle. Everything he saw before made sense now. These men created the right conditions so that humans can flourish on Earth, and when they saw that nature had other plans for the planet, they dropped an asteroid and destroyed any living predator that could erase their experiment for existence. They were always there, always looking, always observing, making sure we would continue existing and evolving. What Nova didn't understand was why these obviously highly intelligent and more than capable persons bothered and spent so much effort and energy in creating something so inferior to them? What was their goal? They needed slaves? They needed humans as organ donners? To prepare the planet so that in the future they could come and collect it as a paid debt? History up to the day had no indications that any of that happened or could happen; on the contrary, rumours of alien abductions and sightings, although they existed, most of the cases were found to be pranks or just lies. Also, Nova knew that the aliens were not either green, nor grey, they didn't have four hands, and they didn't react as animals - aliens are us. If someone is an alien to Earth, it is humans. They were a breed that was brought in a spaceship here. His thoughts were interrupted - that man was there again. He was in that white room. Nova was lost; he couldn't understand what was happening. This time, the feelings were different. This time, he felt that he was there in that room in his physical form and not as a conscience. The man looked at him. Again, he talked to him; he talked in a very calm and almost mesmerizing way.

Man: "I tried to communicate with you through your mind, but when I did, I saw that your brain isn't ready for that. If I even attempted to do that, you would be dead, both here and there. So, I read your mind instead and learnt the language you use to communicate. To be honest, I find it very primitive, but yet attractive, somehow. I never heard my voice before, and it is so curious to feel this sound coming out of me."

Nova: "Am I really here? I mean, okay, I know my consciousness is, but I feel my body as well. If I am here, then back in my time? What is happening there? I exist there? I stopped being? I am confused, and this is actually the first time in my life that I don't know what is happening around me."

Man: "The answer to your question is yes. Yes, you are here and yes, you are there as well. The details of that are not needed. All that is needed is for you to understand I mean you no harm. I want to just talk to you, and then you are free to go and do whatever you wish. Let's start - give me your hands."

Nova, without even thinking about it, gave his hands. When the man touched them, Nova fainted. He was now decanting even deeper into unconsciousness, he felt he was falling but this time he didn't travel alone. The man was with him. They were in a different place in space, they were travelling across galaxies, through black holes. They travelled into deep space, when they suddenly stopped. They were infront of a planet that resembled Earth, but on a closer inspection, it seemed that half of the planet was covered in some sort of metal, the same material that the pyramids were made of. They walked the streets of that planet, and everywhere was metal. The whole place was like it was made in one single cast. People walked the streets as well. They looked alike; perfect bodies, similar clothing. The oldest of them looked a maximum of forty-five years old. Also, the strange thing was that they were all men, no women at all.

Man: "We do not need women. We learned through the centuries to live without them. We are all made in laboratories by semen already preserved millennian ago. I will explain to you why we do not have females amongst us. As you understand, we have powers that none on Earth has, or at least are supposed to have. We have telekinesis, telepathy, we can manipulate every single element of nature, we can create objects with our minds only by having the raw materials in our reach. Each of us has the power alone to destroy a planet. We can make it self-destruct or we can take our time and set it on fire. In agent times, our race ruled everything, and when I say everything, I mean all existence - and trust me, you are not ready for an explanation of what that means. But as every form of power, has its weaknesses, so did ours. Our power comes mainly from our emotions. It was affecting our emotions and our emotions our powers. As we grew in number, and as we conquered more civilizations, we made experiments on ourselves, we unlocked more powers, we grew stronger and became more complex. In the very beginning, we only had telepathy and telekinesis, nothing more of what you have now. As we gain knowledge and power, we noticed that the impact on our emotions was growing as well. It wasn't long until we had the first insistence. Women by nature are more vulnerable to their emotions, more exposed, if you wish. We knew that they were likely to become a liability, but we chose to let things as they were. We needed women for reproduction and for companionship. They were equal to us and they were excellent companions. If it is one thing I miss, it is the touch of a woman. Don't get me wrong, I never saw a woman in my whole life, but we are created and connected in one consciousness, so we share the memories of every ancestor and every single one of us. A woman was pregnant, her body started changing as it is supposed to in order to be prepared and suitable for the new life it will bring. Something went wrong with her pregnancy, nobody knows, it was before the common consciousness, so we only know what the history says about it. And as always, history is based on real events, but it's not real itself, it gets altered and corrupted in the process. So, at some point of the day, without any warning, without any notice, disturbance or indication, just like that, half of our planet was vaporised, gone along with that woman and a lot of our warriors and companions. Those who survived created a shield around the planet and started building it using materials from other planets, mainly the metal material you saw before. The one that we used to build our ships as well, it is called manerioum and it is a flexible living organism. Manerioum, by using the correct amount of electricity, can be shaped as you wish. It is also reusable, and yes, it multiplies itself, as every living creature does. After the first insistence, the council decided to isolate the women and remove as much power as was possible from them. They didn't refuse; they knew that what happened could happen again. They all lost loved ones. They willingly offered their ovum and we kept harvesting from them as much as we could. They are our internal mothers, the last of their kind. We control the process so that only males will come out of it. We controlled the numbers so we will keep our planet sustainable and alive."

Nova: "So, I come from these internal mothers as well? Am I one of you? Am I not human?"

Man: "You are human and all humans are creatures originated by the internal mothers. But as you know now, humans are created in our labs and they are inferior of their creators; although by seeing you here, I realised that we may have underestimated humans a bit."

Nova: "You said the first insistence... there are more?"

Man: "The lack of women and the monotony of being the master of everything wasn't welcomed by all of us. You see, we may be the ultimate creatures, but we have weaknesses, we have personalities, characters, and we have ambitions by nature. When we had no one to conquer, when we had nothing else to learn, no cause in life, we created a cause. We had people demanding that we start destroying civilizations we already had conquered and offered us their recourses. The reason? Their excuse? To do something, just to do something other than just existing. I understand that logic, as I understand the opposite logic. The planet we are now exists only in my memories. This planet was destroyed by civil war. It started without any real excuse, just a small disagreement between two men. No premeditation, nobody planned it, just a small fight which was the spark that everybody was waiting for. The fire started, killings amongst brothers, planets lost, civilizations vanished, galaxies abandoned. When everything settled, and when only a few of us remained alive, we decided that we would be the last of our kind. It was the first time we felt the pain we so easily offered to so many living creatures all over existence. We got two ships that we had stored in a nearby galaxy. We had already arranged for our mother's seeds to be on those ships and we decided to create our species from scratch, but this time, without our abilities. We asked help from other civilizations in order to find and prepare our new home. Of course, they helped us. Don't forget, only one of us was enough to destroy their planet. Also, they were more than ecstatic with our decision. We would be the last of our kind and they could continue living without fear. The rest, you already know - you saw."

Nova: "So, somehow you people thought it will be better to create an inferior-to-you being that looked exactly like you, acted more or less like you, but live less, without any special powers, etc, etc, just to preserve your eternal mother's seeds, and your legacy? Well, I knew God didn't exist, but I never expected our creators to be aliens, so bored that they decided to start a civil war so that they could pass time. So, now you got me here, you showed me everything, you know everything I know, and of course, here comes the million-dollar question. What do you want from me?"

Man: "First, let me give you the full perspective of what is happening here. In your time line, I do not exist. That much I know. I didn't die out of natural causes, as we simply don't die from that. We don't get old, aging stops at some, different for each of us time. We are forever. So, someone or something killed me. I can only locate my existence up to a point and I can access my future as you can access a website, it's like playing a tape fast forward or backward. I can see everything I will see, hear everything I will hear, feel everything I will feel, but I cannot influence anything. It's like watching my life in a monitor. The last thing I remember is me being in my ship, travelling the universe in search of possible new civilizations to study. That's it, that's my last future memory, nothing else, not even how I died, not a clue. In any case, logic says that another one of my race killed me. It was impossible for any other known-to-us species to do that. So, now to what I want from you: I want you to be careful. Your timeline hides dangers and I don't only talk about your brother. I want you to make sure that all our efforts are not to be wasted. I want you to protect our brothers on Earth; they are all that is left from our great civilization. I don't know if anyone else of my kind is yet alive in your timeline, as when we die, we are cut off from the common consciousness. Now, another thing you need to know about humans is this: they have the same potentials as we did, the same brain, the same energy waves, the same psychic potency. But we locked everything, we used selective breeding, chemical castration of your neurons, as well as emotional blocking by modifying your DNA. This is why you get fat, this is why you are hairy, this is why you die, this is why you get sick. We made you weak, we made you fragile, we thought we made you harmless. That was our mistake; we underestimate you. We watched your kind for years, thousands of years. We saw wars, we saw slaughters, we witnessed genocides, we saw you making weapons of mass destruction. You became worse than us, but we chose not to interfere. We were thankful that you hadn't unlocked your potentials. Everything was tolerable, although you were a bloodthirsty kind. You managed to control your nature; you invented politics. That was new for us, but it seemed it worked. Selective manipulation, selective extermination, brutal at the end, but yet controlled. I don't know if anyone else noticed your waking up, as I told you I am cut off our consciousness, but be sure that if any of them are alive, they will come to you. You and your brother are the red line we said we'd never let humans pass. That was the whole point of creating you, that was the epitome of our sacrifice, our loneliness, our cause of existence. Over the years, anomalies were detected, charismatic people, people born with special talents, telekinesis, telepathy, a sort of sixth sense. Some even tried to communicate with us. But none of them were considered dangerous or worthy of our interference. Their brains just had a small percentage more capacity than the other humans, but yet extraordinary for the rest of humanity. Some of them were considered holy, sons of Gods, divine. Most of them founded the main religions people on Earth follow. Charismatic people, but nothing to be compared with you. If we knew about you, at least if I knew about you, I would have made sure that we would have interfered. One way or the other, your presence on Earth would be discontinued. Now, my friend, back to you and your brother. I have no clue how they managed to unlock your potentials, no idea if you were born like that, if you were bred, if they created you from scratch, no idea at all. All I know is that you two are the most dangerous beings that ever lived on Earth. As I understand, you personally are generally peaceful in nature, not violent. Actually, what I am surprised about is that you have feelings for people. You cherish material things, you managed somehow to keep your mental world in order, you found your order in your chaos. Your brother, on the other hand, he is so different. He is dangerous, unstable, gets lost in his feelings. He seems to be hashed treaded. I have no idea what he wants from you, I cannot predict. I cannot help you on that, no advice to give, just be careful and don't trust him. Keep in mind that he cannot find you here and he will never know what you did and saw here. He used that poor man to send you a message, but I used that message to get you here. We are cut off from anything and anyone, here it is just you and me. Now, my brother, I will release you. You go back, you go and be. Good luck, and remember the burden you have on your shoulders. Also, remember that your brother may not be your greatest worry or enemy; good chances are that one of us may come for you and your brother."

Nova woke up. He was on a hospital bed, monitors all around him accompanied with that awful smell that all hospitals have in common, Dr Stan was sleeping on a couch next to him with an empty bottle of scotch in his hands. At the end of the room, he noticed Dr Lee taking some notes. The room was huge; it was made of glass and it was inside of another room. Nova understood that he was in a room made of lead. He had heard of this room before. He was briefed and knew about it, but had never visited it. This room was created when they discovered that One escaped his captivity. It was designed in such a way that any brain and psychic waves were blocked. It was designed so that One would lose track of Nova's whereabouts.

Nova: "I would either like a package of painkillers, or some of the leftover scotch. Or even better, both of them, please. My head feels like a thousand kilos of trash."

Dr Lee: "I see you kept your humour - bad humour, but yet humour. Welcome, back my friend, you've been out for six days and fourteen hours. Long sleep, even for you. So, I was wondering what dreams you had? Anything interesting? Wanna share with us?"

Nova: "First, I was not joking, I need a box of painkillers and that bottle. Second, nice to be back, Doctor. Third, I feel like I haven't slept for a year. Fourth, if you want to know about my dreams, go back to number one…"

Dr Stan: "I thought I missed you. Well, I didn't. Thank you for clearing my thoughts on that. Here is the bottle, enjoy. As far as the painkillers, that's Dr Lee's job."

Dr Lee gives him a box of painkillers. He took a full hand of them and put them in his mouth, then he took the bottle and drank all the scotch that Dr Stan had spared. About ten minutes passed and then Nova broke his silence.

Nova: "You really wanna know what dreams I saw? I don't remember a lot, all I remember is that I was back at my house with you, Dr Lee, playing our game of chess, only this time we continued our game in the bed."

Dr Stan: "Wait… you mean you two haven't made it yet? But I thought…"

Dr Lee: "Doctor, that night Nova told you we were playing chess, we actually just played chess and I have the feeling that Nova let me win in order to get me in bed, but obviously he has a lot to figure out about women. But as you both know - well, Nova knows better than you - I am clear with my sexual preferences. I prefer a beautiful female body than a hairy masculine body. I wonder what other women find in men. I mean, you are just oversized children with hairs everywhere, and don't get me started on the rest of your belongings…"

Nova: "I did let you win, that's true, but I did it because I am a gentleman, not because I needed anything from you."

They all laughed, until suddenly the atmosphere of the room went from joyful to cold and dark. They all had questions and worries and none of them knew how to start or what to say. The two doctors knew that Nova was lying. During the time he was out he was deeply monitored and his brainwaves and heart beats showed that he was experiencing something intense. The numbers were off the charts. If he was a normal human, his brain would have ceased functioning and his heart would have exploded in his chest. Nova knew their thoughts; after his trip and what he saw and learned, he decided to turn his powers on, and for the first time in a lot of time, he did what he promised to himself not to do again. He was spying his friends. He felt bad because he knew he didn't play fair and that he violated their trust, but he felt he had no alternative. He now acknowledged the danger that he, his brother, and any potential alien could bring to this world. He had lost the luxury of just trusting people. He decided to put his guard on and be cautious with every simple move he made.

Nova: "So, doctors, when will I get out of this hole? I feel great, the pills really did the job. You should have tried this combination days ago, Doctor."

Dr Stan: "Nova, I sense something different in you. Are you reading our minds? Something worries you; what happened, why you lost your senses, what you saw? From your readings, we know that something happened. I'm not buying that you don't remember anything. You remember how many whiskeys I had ten years ago this day, even though you were supposed to be unconscious."

Nova: "My friend, I really need to get out of here. I need fresh air; this room is depressing. If there is something that you really need to know, you will. But all in good time. Now please, get me out of here."

Dr Stan stood there for a minute. He took out his tabaco holder, a silver one with a blue cross in the middle. He took a cigarette, put it in his mouth, lit it up, scratched his head and turned to Dr Lee.

Dr Stan: "Doctor, as I understand, this is a no smoking area, so how about me and my friend have our smoke outside?"

Dr Lee smiled, started taking all the monitoring equipment off Nova's body, and brought him a black bathrobe and a pair of slippers. He got dressed really quickly, and within minutes the two men were in the elevator heading up.

Nova: "So all these days you were here? On the couch? Really? You were afraid that I would leave you? I would never do this to you. You will receive a letter from my lawyer first." He laughed loud while he lit up his cigarette.

Dr Stan: "I preferred staying here rather than back at the office. I get paid monthly and not by tasks. So yes, I preferred taking a few days off and staying away from everything. So don't flatter yourself; you offered me free vacations and a very good couch to sleep on. Actually, that couch is much better than my own bed. And if you want to leave, nobody will stop you, you know that. Also, when and if you do leave, please give your brother my regards."

The two men spent a couple of hours in the car, just driving around listening to music, talking about everything that came to their minds. Of course, the good doctor had a stash of scotch in his car and he shared some of it with his friend. As they were driving around in the Doctor's grey Bentley Continental GT, listening to jazz, having each a bottle of scotch in their hands and smoking fine cigars, Nova found himself in a mixture of feelings. He felt guilt, as although he pretended to enjoy the conversation with the Doctor, he could not. He already knew every word and every thought in his mind before even being in the process of vocalisation. He also felt worried, stressed and shocked. He thought he knew everything about the world, he thought the complicated word was simple. It was not; it was beyond any imagination. The nature that ruled the planet did so only because it was allowed to do so. God was a man in a strange tight outfit who resembled more of an ancient Greek demigod than Buddha, Jesus, Allah or any other claimed God. Suddenly, his thoughts were interrupted. They entered a basement parking lot, and the Doctor took out of his pocket a small gadget with a smaller screen. He put his fingerprint at the screen, then his tongue. Suddenly, the area where the Bentley was parked started to move. They were moving down on earth. After a few minutes, they stopped. They were in a huge concrete area that resembled a military hangar. People in military outfits were moving all over the area, huge screens were on the walls, some showing direct video screens, and others, reports from satellites.

Dr Stan: "Here is our house for the next few... actually, who knows until when. We are going to stay here until we locate and capture or destroy One."

Nova knew that they never intended to capture his brother, the order was one and only one: destroy the target by any means necessary. He looked around and started walking towards a closed steel door.

Dr Stan: "Well, it seems you know your way around here, that is actually your room, but it seems you already knew that, didn't you?"

Nova looked back at him, tried to smile but he couldn't. He turned back again and entered his room. The Doctor knew that he was hiding something, he knew that something changed, and he was worried if what changed was for the best or worse. He felt he lost any control he had over him, he felt fear for the first time. He had noticed in the past that Nova was growing, his character was evolving, but all those changes were in a relevantly normal and expected frame. He tried to empty his brain and stop analysing. He knew he was naked; he knew he was watched, monitored, he didn't know how to react. He entered his Bentley, took out that gadget, put his finger and his tongue on it, and then he scrolled the menu. He chose and pushed a button: 'sleep'. Nova's room slowly but steadily released a chemical, it was the same chemical used to hypnotize him days ago. The Doctor left the building the same way he entered it. After a few minutes he was back at his office; he was again in that room, sitting in front of a big black screen, when suddenly a voice came through.

Voice 4: "What is it, Doctor? Why this sudden call, anything knew? We were updated about Nova's health and his whereabouts."

Dr Stan: "Gentlemen, just let me tell you that in order for me to be here, I used the 'sleep' option."

Silence in the room for a few seconds - dead silence, not even background sounds, not even the usual noise of the Doctor smoking.

Voice 3: "You have our attention, Doctor."

Voice 4: "It seems we lost all possible control, otherwise you would never have used that option. We know that you and him are close and you consider him a friend. We also aware that you risked everything in order to be here, so I believe I talked on all of our behalves when I say, we are all ears and no mouths."

Dr Stan: "Nova, after his fight with Captain, fell into a comma for days; you know that as well as all the relevant details, as well as his medical and unusual reports. I am convinced he unlocked all or some of his powers. Whatever he experienced changed him. I don't know if the change is for good or bad, or if he is feeling in danger or lost his trust for us. The fact is that he unlocked something and that's not what worries me - what worries me is that he is hiding it. Also, the presence of Captain makes no sense. One is not a fool and he is a deadly, sophisticated and calculative machine. He could have killed him back on Pole as he did with the rest of ZEUS. He also knew as a fact that he was not a match for Nova. With or without his full potential Nova is a superhuman, a mere human with enhanced muscle power and speed was not enough to kill Nova. If killing him is the target, then Captain could never be the tool of his doom, and the fact that immediately after Nova had entered Captain's brain he collapsed, or to be more accurate, entered into a trance, reveals something else.

Something that Nova wishes to hide from us, from me, something worth the risk I took by putting him to sleep. As you understand, everything changed. I cannot say he is a liability; I say that we need to decide how we treat him, how we choose to act based on our new facts."

Voice 2: "I guess due to the fact that we have his brother spreading terror, and with unknown motives and cause, leaving Nova to sleep is not a solution, so not incapacitating him either."

Voice 1: "Can we reboot him?"

Dr Stan: "We couldn't control him when he was an infant, not now that he is far more experienced and alerted."

Voice 3: "How about confronting him? If things are the way you say, then he already knows we are on him. If he has showed anything to us, it is that he loves his lifestyle and that he respects life. Yes, I understand that he is changed, but think about it; he woke up, had his scotch with a bunch of pills and had a ride with you. If he wished to harm us, or escape, he could have done so with extreme ease. So, let's just talk to him. It's not wise, anyway, to try and hide from him. He can be in our minds as a parasite without us even knowing he is there."

Voice 4: "I believe there is no certainty in any decision we make today. Every outcome is possible, so any decision we make, as long as it is a common one, will be the correct one. I vote we all talk to him, confront him, be straight with him as we always have been. Now I am thinking about it, we never had any option to begin with."

Voice 1: "I agree."

Voice 2: "Agree."

Voice 3: "Let's try it."

Dr Stan: "I will make the arrangements."

The screens went dark again. The Doctor stayed for a few hours in the dark room, he continued with his scotch, he opened the last draw of his desk and took out an album. It was an album full of happy moments of his common life with his former fiancée. For the first time after a period of many years he felt remorse, felt he had lost control of his life. All those sacrifices, the hours at the laboratory, the office, all of those conventional career opportunities he lost. His future marriage, the only woman he actually loved, all for the project, a project who got a name, a project who became his friend, a friend who lied to him, a lost project. He was always the one who stood up wherever he was, at the school, army, university, the one with the most beautiful women by his side, the one with the scholarships, the career opportunities, the one who attracted success. He remembered the day that he first heard about Nova, who was then called just 'Project'. He was teaching at the university. His class was full of young women, he was wearing a black bespoke suit with a white shirt and no tie, his Rolex and his blue glasses, and he was explaining the theory of evolution when the door opened - it was the dean. That was highly unusual; he never ever entered a class room. He actually never left his office.

Dean: "Class, this session is over, you are released for the rest of the day. Doctor, please, I need you in my office limitedly."

Dr Stan waved positively with his head and started packing his bag. He was wondering what had happened. Is it possible that one of his students with whom he had an affair talked? There was no other obvious explanation. It must be the blonde one, what was her name? The one that told me she loved me, the one that dropped university so she could forget about me.

Maria, yes, that was her name. She did it, she actually did what she promised me, she destroyed me. My teaching career is over. Who would want a professor who has sexual intercourse with his students? He continues thinking of any possible excuse he could give so he could at least get a chance to keep his job. Suddenly, he found himself in front of the Dean's office door. It was open; inside was the Dean sitting at his office, he noticed one man and a woman both dressed in black suits sitting opposite the dean. He thought they were either Maria's lawyers or her parents. He entered the room. He was waiting for any of them to say something, he needed them to initiate the conversation and clarify the reason he was called. He avoided to give the stigma of the conversation that will follow. Then the Dean broke the silence.

Dean: "Doctor, please close the door behind you." Dr Stan did so. "I would like you to meet two other doctors: Dr Lee, a specialist in psychology and hypnosis, and Dr Nicholas, a specialist in neurology and brain functioning. Now, these people came here directly from the government. They are also good friends of our sponsors here at the university. They would like to have a word with you. As I am instructed, the nature of the conversation is such that I am not allowed to be present, so I will leave you alone. Oh, and Stan, I hope you are not in trouble, and further on I hope our sponsorships are not in any way compromised, because if that is the case, I promise you that there will be not one university in the whole world that will ever accept you for anything else except as a janitor."

The Dean left his office, leaving all three doctors standing in the middle of the room. Dr Stan was confused; he now knew that this had nothing to do with Maria or any other mischief he had ever done during his career. This was much more important, way more serious and certainly more interesting. He reached out his hand and shook the hands of the two doctors. He then took a good look at them from the bottom up, certainly their salary was way higher than his.

Dr Lee: "You must be very confused about our visit here. Don't worry, this has nothing to do with Maria or any of your other mistresses. Our visit here comes with an offer, an offer of a lifetime. No details will be revealed to you before you have accepted and signed an NDA agreement."

Dr Nicholas: "We are assembling a group of specialists in order to study and prepare a unique project. A project like no other, a project so well kept that not even the congress or the president have the details we are willing to share with you. What made us turn our attention to you was your thesis about the human brain and its restrictions. We found it fascinating; the idea alone that human brains are restrained by a mechanism that forbids and minimizes its full capacity and capabilities is extraordinary."

Dr Stan: "Well, thanks for the compliments, but you must know that my thesis was the reason that I wasn't taken seriously by most of my fellow professors. And you must also know that I earned the nickname Professor X for that. I was taken seriously only when I renounced my previous thesis with a new one, which claimed that the human brain is already evolved to its maximum capacity and that the rest of the brain that is not used is actually a remnant of evolution. In any case, what exactly have you come here to offer me?"

Dr Nicholas: "We came here to tell you that your original thesis is correct, and we are here to offer you the privilege to work with a person that knows no restrictions, whose brain lacks any barriers and who needs our help."

Dr Lee: "You understand that any further details will only be revealed when you accept our offer."

Dr Stan: "I haven't heard an offer yet, I just heard you people talking about something that I admit sounds fascinating and I would not lie, I am intrigued. But as you know, I have a life, I have a professorship here, I earn good money, I am engaged, and although as you obviously know I had my affairs, I love her. You are asking me to work on a deep state secret, to sign an NDA, and as I understand, have my life monitored just in case I give up any secrets. You are asking me to lie about my work to my fiancée, to my friends, to everybody and also put myself in danger as it is expected in such situations. What do you offer in return?"

Dr Lee: "You don't seem to understand. This is actually an offer you cannot refuse. We are either here to take your positive answer or to accuse you officially of your affairs with your students. You see, people saw us here; we must give an excuse. The excuse is either that we came here to offer you a job at pentagon, or to investigate the allegations against you."

Dr Stan: "That's blackmail. What will you get if you destroy me? I will never be able to work again, my fiancé will leave me, I will face criminal and civil sanctions. You expect me to smile and just say yes, I am in?"

Dr Nicholas: "This piece of paper mentions some of the benefits of working for us, and when I mean us, I do not necessarily mean the government. The government is the weakest party of this alliance."

Dr Nicholas handed Dr Stan a piece of paper. It mentioned his monthly salary, which was way more than his now yearly gross income, and a written immunity by the government concerning any criminal or civil fault he may fall into during his employment. Exceptions of course existed, and they were orientated around high treason, selling or giving state secrets, etc, etc. The list of benefits was huge and it included private jets, freedom of choosing his staff, tax free income, etc, etc. Dr Stan smiled and looked at the other doctors.

Dr Stan: "It seems that you two need to work on your presentation a little bit. You should have started with this and the rest would be unnecessary."

There in that office, Dr Stan's life changed for ever. He signed all the documents given to him, and he also signed his resignation. He was told that his employment started immediately and that the next morning he should present himself at that psychiatric institution in Boston USA. He will never forget his first day there, the first day he saw Nova. He was welcomed by Dr Lee, he passed through security, the hidden elevators, and he finally reached the laboratory. Dr Nicholas was there waiting for them. He shaked Dr Stan's hand, smiled at Dr Lee, and asked them to join him as he was walking towards the room where Nova was held.

Dr Nicholas: "Dr Stan, have you ever met a GOD? Neither have I, but I'll show you the closest thing to a GOD."

The big tank of amniotic fluid rose up, and in it was a man, not much younger than Dr Stan, maybe five years younger. Attached to him were the same wires and monitors as many years later. Dr Stan was stunned. He felt immediately the room atmosphere becoming heavier, the temperature and his mood dropping. He felt he was being watched, and he had feelings he could not explain, all this without any obvious reason. All of that happened the moment the tank came up from the place it was kept in the ground. The young man in the tank was in his early twenties, and his hair was almost as long as his height, black thick hair, his body perfect in every aspect. Dr Stan understood that he was the project. He was the reason he was there.

Dr Nicholas: "Meet project G.O.D, an abbreviation for Genetically Orientated Deviants. All its details will be given to you today and you will have all the necessary time to study it."

Dr Stan: "He is a human being."

Dr Nicholas: "Sorry?"

Dr Stan: "You repeatedly said PROJECT. Well, I don't care in what way he is different from us, how special he is and what exactly your plans are for him. But he is a human being. I don't want to hear anyone referring to him as if he is an object again. This poor person is trapped in an amniotic pool for us to study. I am not aware yet why he is here and what we want from him, but he is a HE. Understood?"

Dr Nicholas: "Whatever makes you happy."

Dr Stan walked into his office, looked around and noticed the luxury of the room. It was dressed in oak. The desk was a big Victorian one, obviously an antique, and instead of windows it had big paintings or renaissance. On the desk, a pile of files and a last generation mac PC. He thought the people who paid for it had both good taste and unlimited funds. He sat on his chair, noticed a bottle of a fifty-year-old Balvenie and a crystal glass next to it, opened the bottle, smelled it, and put a generous dose in his glass. He started drinking while reading the files. As he read, the more whiskey he consumed, he started having second thoughts of his presence there, but he knew there was no way out for him. He couldn't just get up and leave, he was already too deep. His thoughts continued travelling him back to the very first day he was put infront of that big black screen. He remembered Dr Lee and Dr Nicholas calling him. He turned and he saw them along with all the other doctors who one way or the other worked on project G.O.D.

Dr Lee: "Come with us, our sponsors would like to talk to all. As I understand, this is the first time you will 'meet them', so I will give you a very short briefing as we are supposed to be in the briefing room in fifteen minutes. First rule: you don't ask anything about them. It's four of them, we have no idea who they are. They appear in a big dark split screen; their voices are changed. We don't know if they are men, women, politicians, entrepreneurs, or even if they actually exist. Rule number two: their decisions concerning the project are always taken unanimously and we have no saying on them. All four of them must agree or disagree with our suggestions or proposals. Rule number three: remember rule number one and two."

The group of scientists kept walking until they reached the room. Dr Stan was there for the first time. The room was huge, a big glass conference table with eighteen chairs, all white, a bar on the corner and a huge screen that took all the eastern wall. Each of them took one chair and Dr Nicholas took the head of the table. Dr Stan headed to the bar and poured a glass of scotch, then went and took the one seat left. The room got dark. The screen lit the room a bit, but not much, as it was just showing a black screen divided in four images. Dr Nicholas stood up and looked at everybody looking at him, then addressed to the big screen.

Dr Nicholas: "Gentlemen, as you can see, we are all here and all in time. I would like to..."

He was brutally interrupted by a voice that came out of every corner of the room as speakers were installed all over it.

Voice 1: "Thank you, Dr Nicholas, we haven't brought you here for a discussion or for a briefing. We will only take a minute of your precious time, as we brought you here for an announcement."

Voice 2: "Dr Nicholas, please exchange places with Dr Stan."

Dr Nicholas was shocked. He knew that the head chair was always given to the head scientist, the one who took all the difficult and important decisions about project G.O.D. He also knew that the decision was taken and he had no choice and no way to appeal it. Although he felt insulted by the way he was demoted, he just went over Dr Stan, looked at him in the eyes and with a very cold tone in his voice, told him 'the chair is yours'. Dr Stan was new there, he knew nothing about the hierarchy or what that chair meant. He thought that the sponsors just wanted to have a better look at him as he was the new guy. He took his glass and moved to the head of the table, sat on the chair, and noticed everybody looking at him except Dr Nicholas.

Voice 3: "You all know what that means; you are taking our orders from Dr Stan, now. You are all released and free to go back at your tasks."

Voice 4: "All except you, Dr Stan. Take that bottle you opened and come back to your place. We have a lot to discuss."

Although Dr Stan wasn't expecting what just happened, he didn't look shocked, either. He just kept drinking his scotch and waited for the four mysterious benefactors to talk to him and set up the pace of the conversation.

Voice 4: "Cheers, Doctor, I am enjoying one right now. I am happy to see a man who knows how to enjoy the little treasures of life. But as you should have already figured out, we are all extremely busy and important persons. We don't have all the time in the world but the current time. This project is the most important investment we have. So, whenever you need us, you just push the dial button on the mobile phone that is already in your office, sitting on your expensive desk. It only calls on one encrypted number, and is useless in every other aspect. After the call ends, in a few seconds, a minute at the most, you will receive to your personal phone a message with the details of our communication. Now if we need you, we will find a way to reach you, for that be sure and have no worries about."

Voice 1: "As a head of this project, you will know more than the rest. The first thing you need to now is this: all of them believe that Dr Noe, your predecessor, died in a car accident. That is a lie - he was murdered. We managed to save his family and take them somewhere safe, but it was too late for him. We found him brutally beaten with his head cut off his body. He was found in the backyard of his house. Thank God nobody was home. We knew something was wrong hours before his death. Each one of you is equipped with a microchip; only the heads of the project know about this. It follows and records all of your vitals as well as your current location. In your case, the scotch you found in your office was the vehicle that delivered you the microchip - you swallowed it. Now, back to Dr Noe. That day, we noticed he changed his routine back home, as well as the changes in his vitals. We tried to locate him but after a few minutes we lost signal. Whoever did it was a professional with huge funds. We believe it was our Russians friends, as we believe they tried to get as much information as possible out of him. We have no idea if they succeeded or not. So, you do understand the position you are in, as well you understand that it is you who actually put yourself in this position."

Dr Stan lit up another cigarette and filled up his glass again. He was shocked, confused, scared and hopeless, but he did not allow his face to show any of that. He kept calm and knew the only way through this was to play along.

Dr Stan: "Does Nicholas is aware of any of that? Actually, does anybody else know?"

Voice 1: "No, Dr Nicholas was a very temporary solution until we found you. Believe it or not, you were selected many years ago. We always have a line of succession for everyone here, even the janitor. Don't make the next question, you will get no answer. You are here to listen and not to talk."

Voice 2: "For now, that is. Now, Dr Stan, take the rest of the day off. Go home, relax, take your decisions always considering your new realities, and come back again tomorrow fresh."

The screen went blank, the lights came back, and Dr Stan was still sitting there. He stayed there until the bottle got empty, then he went out of the premisses, not noticing and not answering to all the people who tried to congratulate him. He took his Porsche, lit a cigarette, and in thirty minutes was home. She was waiting for him. He loved her so much that in order to protect her he did what he had to do. When she saw him, her face shined. She didn't expect him home so soon. She went to him, hugged him, kissed him, but something was different; he was different, he was dark.

Nicky: "Honey, what happened? Everything okay at work? Did you have a fight with someone? Please don't look at me like that, I know you. Something really serious happened. Talk to me, please."

Dr Stan: "Please have a sit; we need to talk. Yesterday, I gave my resignation from the university. Lately, I've not been doing okay, although you will probably say that you know me and you haven't noticed anything. Well, I was visiting a psychologist. I am diagnosed with depression and I've also been taking pills for a couple of months already. After long sessions and a lot of Valium, I came to an understanding. I need changes in my life. I wasn't happy, and that had to do with every aspect of my life. I am still under medication, I am yet visiting the psychiatrist, I am yet depressed and yet not happy with my life. What I am trying to say is that I need some time alone, some time to figure things out, time to heal and find my way."

Nicky: "I had no idea, baby. I understand, I will give you as much space as you need, I will not bother you. If you need anything or anyone to talk to, I will be here in minutes. We can get through this. Fuck your job, if it made you unhappy then we'll have to find something else. We have money, I have money, I will work for both of us. We will make some smart economy and we will handle everything, as long as we have each other."

Dr Stan felt like somebody took his heart out and stepped on it. He felt the love coming towards him, and he knew that what he was hearing was genuine; it came from her soul. He also felt the agony in her voice. He understood that she would do anything to be with him. At that moment, his heart was already broken - he would never be the same again. He just realised how much he cherished the life he had, he now understood what he was about to lose. The value of his daily routine, the value of having a loving face to come back to every night. He had regretted the choice he had made the previous day, if you can actually call it a choice. He regretted his adulteries, those empty moments, he regretted allowing his ego and his desires to drag him down. He had the perfect life. There existed no car, no house, no boat, no bank account more luxurious and necessary than his daily routine, more comfortable than the couch he used to sit on at nights enjoying his scotch and cigar, while having Nicky's head on his laps. He took a big breath and did what he thought should be done.

Dr Stan: "Nicky, I also need to confess something else. I cheated on you, repeatedly. I am sorry, but I did. All those trips for conferences, meetings, publishers, in each one of them I was accompanied by other women. Sometimes one, and some other times two. This is who I am. I'm sorry, but you deserve better."

Nicky: "You are lying, I know you are. You would never do that to me. I know you love me; I know you care, I can feel it, I can see it every time I catch you looking at me. I understand you are under medication and you need your space. I will leave you alone until you feel better and then we can talk about our future, your professional dreams, anything you like."

Dr Stan was actually expecting that reaction. She cherished their life, she invested in him, she gave everything for him, she was always there. She wouldn't just leave without a fight. So, he did something that would destroy every person in her place: he took out his mobile phone, he entered the photos folder, put in a code, and gave her the phone. There was a ton of pictures with him with other women; some pictures taken in public, restaurants, pubs, clubs, and some others were more personal, as some of the women in the pictures were either naked or in their underwear. She said no word, she put the mobile on the table, she kissed Dr Stan on the forehead, she took her bag, and left. She never came back to get her stuff, she never called, he never saw her. He did what he believed was the best for both of them. She wasn't any longer in any danger, and he was free to do his job without abstractions. That night, he cried, he cried so much that his eyes dried, but somehow, he kept crying. He slept on the floor, destroyed by wrong decisions, alcohol and guilt.

The next morning, he woke with a terrible headache. He took almost a box of painkillers and went into the shower. He put on the grey suit he loved, his favourite black shoes, chose a blue tie, put on his good watch, and left the house. The man that came out of that door that morning was a different man, a cold man, a man that made a choice, a man that killed his remorse so he can tolerate his own existence. He chose to live without feelings, or at least with the least possible feelings a human being could have.

Dr Stan got out of his reminisce, it was time to leave, he put the album back, stood up, took the keys of his Bentley and left the premises. He was now driving back to Nova. He knew what he had to do, or at least he was aware of his only option. He had no choice than to play all or nothing. He was ready for it, he had sacrificed his whole life for this, he was going to make sure that his sacrifices were not vain. He was already in the basement, Nova was there standing and smiling, he wasn't in capitated as he was supposed to. He was wearing a black suit with a red tie and he had his shades already on, he was waiting for him.

Nova: "I'm ready to go. Oh, and on our way to your office, please make a stop at the cigar shop. I'm short…"

Dr Stan: "So, you decided to come clean?"

Nova: "No, you decided to come clean…"

The two men walked together and got in the car. Nova decided to drive and Dr Stan was happy for that. He preferred to have his mind as focused as possible so he could find a way to make this discussion.

Dr Stan: "So? How we going to do this? I know you are unlocked, that much is shown. I feel stupid even talking to you as you know what I'm about to say before I even say it. You know that's not fair."

Nova: "No, Doctor, I will tell you what's not fair; to be in a fucking fluid for thirty-five years, not being able to move, but having full awareness, that's not fair. Also, not fair is not having a childhood although you understand what that is, my childhood memories never existed, so I borrowed some from all of you people. Not fair is to have your character downloaded into you by a fucking USB, and you know what else is not fair? To consider you the only real friend I have, and not to be able to understand if the way I feel about you is because I want to feel it, or because I was supposed to, because of that bloody USB that infused me your problematic character. Oh, and another thing; not fair is to finally having your existence more or less sorted out, and then your psychopath superman brother appears from nowhere and hunting you down for reasons you don't know or understand. And having that psychopath brother of yours sending you subconscious messages with a raised and bred killer."

Dr Stan: "Yes, that sounds not fair. Everything you said except my character. You should be grateful you did not get Dr Nicholas' character, as that was the other option."

Nova: "Yes, getting that would be a disaster. Imagine me as Nicholas with all the powers I have, those that I know about and those that remain hidden and unknown. I would be the biggest jackass in the whole universe. My ego would be larger than the universe, actually, no place to put my ego. Anyway, Doctor, as you suspect, I have released my powers. I don't feel very comfortable by doing so, but I have good reasons; my brother is only one of them. The other reasons are not for you to know yet."

Dr Stan: "Please tell me, are you in my mind now?"

Nova: "Nope, I was there before."

Dr Stan: "When before?"

Nova: "Before, you know, when you thought you'd drugged me. You can only do that once, you know. My body and brain analysed the synthesis of that drug the first time. I discovered that I can create antibodies and antidotes for anything I came in contact with. You see, I keep getting better and stronger. So yes, I was in your brain before. I also was in your four shady friends' brains. You would not believe who they actually are. But I know that you knowing that would put you in unbelievable danger. Also, keep in mind that their motives are not purely economic as you always believed. But okay, that's not our priority now."

Dr Stan: "What is our priority, my friend?"

Nova: "Our priority is to make sure that the balance of the universe stays as it is. Let's just say that I have reasons to believe that my brother is not the most dangerous person who ever existed, or exists. I need to find a place where I can practice, a place where there will be no danger to hurt anyone. From the day I released my brain, I keep feeling things. It's like something was born inside me, something that tries to get out, and the way I am right now, if that something emerges, I will not be able to control it. My senses are more acute, I can see for miles, I can focus on every possible detail, and I can use my hearing to listen, even the noise of an insect flying miles away. My smell? That's the worst. I can smell shit, Doctor, in a way nobody should ever smell it. After I woke up from the coma, I got an attack from my senses, they overwhelmed me. I more or less controlled it up until we went to the bunker. When I was left alone, I lost control of my body. I could not focus my sights, my sense of smell, my hearing; it was so confusing I thought I was going to die. Fortunately, when you used that drug, my brain and body focused on that, tried to figure out the formula to get rid of it. During those seconds I managed to control all of my senses. You see, I'm an easy learner. Thanks for that, Doctor."

Dr Stan: "Glad to know I helped. Now, I will not insist for you to give me any insights into what happened during those six days, but I know you are doing what you believe is the best. You got that from me…"

Nova: "So, any place for me to play with my super powers?"

Dr Stan: "So, we are not going to meet with our four friends?"

Nova: "Nope."

Dr Stan: "Okay, I will update them and tell them that you'll be at the Nevada nuclear testing area, playing with yourself."

Nova left Dr Stan outside of his house. He took the Bentley, went to a superstore, and got a sleeping bag, supplies, and a lot of alcohol and cigars. The next time the two men would meet, one of them would be a different person.

Meanwhile, One was already in the USA. He was shaved now, had a ponytail holding his long white hair, and his eyes red as always. He was wearing just a pair of black jeans and some military type boots. He was outside of the psychiatric clinic in Boston where he was spotted by the surveillance cameras. Immediately, soldiers came out of everywhere. Helicopters with snipers were above him, and the whole facility transformed; armoured covers dropped in front of the windows and barb wires dropped from the roof top on the perimeter of the building. Security personnel were on the streets moving people away from the area. He was expected; they didn't know the day or time, but they knew they were a possible target. He did kill all the Russians scientists that were involved in his project, it only made sense to come for their American counterparts. It was like he wanted to erase his recorded existence - now he was there to do the same for his brother. He wasn't surprised at all. He felt their presence there long before he was even close. He stood outside of the building. His head never moved. He didn't need to see everyone's exact location; his senses worked as a sonar. He was all over the place, he had a full 360-degree awareness. He felt their heart beats, their breathing, he was already inside their minds. He made one step forward and until he made the next step a barrage of gunshots was heard. Two helicopters fell from the sky, and all the men dropped dead by their own guns, he made them kill themselves. As he made the third step, the reenforced door that was standing in front of him just melted. He kept walking and as he passed bellow the melted door, melting iron dropped on him - but it didn't hurt him, it didn't even touch his skin. It just kept falling like a drop of water does when it falls on a freshly polished car. He was now inside. All the electronics of the building just fried, the lights exploded, and it was pitch dark, but he could see. His vision was as good in pure black as it was in the daylight, it was excellent. He reached the toilets, the entrance of the elevator opened wide. The elevator was down at its final destination, as the last person who used it was already down in the laboratory. Without even thinking about it, he just jumped, his unnatural moves, where executed naturally as they were the most natural thing in the world. He landed on the elevator's top, and then, with a touch of his right palm, the elevator's top steel section was blown and gave away; it just fell down and touched the bottom steel part of the elevator. He kept walking. The personnel were hiding, some of them in the closet, others in the big refrigerators of the lab, some others in their offices. As he kept walking, people around him vaporised; in the closet, in the fridges, in the offices, one after the other just ceased existing. The only thing that was left out of them was a black shadow, that was his trademark after all. One looked around, went into Dr Stan's office, opened the last draw of his office and took his photo album. He then just left. When he was finally out of there, the building just burst in fire. He kept walking in the streets when a big M1 Abrams blocked his way. The tank was at a distance of about twenty metres from him, when without warning, the tank shot an M830 round against him. The round stopped a few metres away from him, and as it stopped it started to dismantle, piece by piece, bolts and screws. Within seconds the whole round was a bunch of parts laying on the ground. One took a look at the tank and the tank exploded and blew into pieces, the persons inside and the tanks steel became one and the same. The man in charge of the whole operation gave an order of retreat; nobody was to try and engage with him, no more unnecessary deaths. He just kept walking, he had the same pace, as if he was alone and just going for a casual walk. During this whole process he never changed his pace, he never even blinked. It was clear to everybody now that he wasn't going to be stopped by conventional warfare weapons. As he was leaving the scene, he walked next to soldiers who just didn't have the time and luxury of leaving the place. He walked by them like they were not even there. He gave them as much attention as you give to a piece of sand when you walk on a beach. They were just there, insignificant, nothing, at least nothing worth his time and attention. He was monitored and watched via two spy satellites as he was leaving the scene, at least now they could have a sight on his whereabouts. Suddenly he stopped, turned his head to the sky, and then kept walking. The satellite's electrical wiring was fried, then the order was given: stop following him. No attempts shall be made to intercept or even record his whereabouts. Just let him go - we lost enough men today. The soldiers left behind couldn't comprehend what just happened; they were all elites, they had all faced the hell of war, they had all took lives, they had felt the pain of loss before, but this... this was different. This, they could not explain or even start to give reason to.

Meanwhile, Dr Stan's phone wrang. It was an unknown caller. He thought twice about answering it - it was like he knew something was wrong. He had a strange feeling of despair and it had nothing to do with Nova leaving him. He finally answered the phone.

Dr Stan: "Stan here, who is it?"

It was the voice of a man he never heard before, but somehow, he knew he had talked to him in the pass, his tone and use of language seemed familiar. The man's voice was nervous and stressful. He was sure now that something really bad had occurred.

Man on the phone: "Doctor, we have a situation. We are all in danger; we need to lay low until we see what can be done."

Dr Stan: "Who is it?"

Man on the phone: "You know who I am, although this is the first time you have heard my normal voice. We've talked numerous times during the last years. I was the one on the top left of your screen."

Dr Stan got the chills. It was the man he only knew as Voice 1. He was calling him from a conventional cell phone, which meant something went really bad, something terrible had happened. His mind went to Nova.

Dr Stan: "Sir, is Nova okay? What's wrong? What happened? Why have you called me on my phone?"

The man explained to him what had just happened at the laboratory, the number of casualties, the enormous power of One, and the fact that he disappeared and his whereabouts were unknown.

Man on the phone: "He is killing everyone who had anything to do with him and his brother. He is erasing their scientific footprint. Our records are not enough for him; he needs our memories, our knowledge, and our actions erased, as well. You understand that we are all as good as dead. I've contacted the other three. They are heading as we talk to supposedly safe places, if such a thing exists that is. As far for me, I am doing the same. I suggest you too do the same; you were the closest person to his brother. You are the head of the project; it would make no sense to let you live. I am actually surprised he didn't kill you first. This being is not human, he is the devil with superman powers, a maniac, a killing machine with a goal. He has a plan - what plan, I know not, but what I know is that the current step of that plan is our elimination. This may be the last time we talk, Doctor. I called you to warn you and to tell you something you need to know. Something personal. He took that album you thought you'd hid in your office drawer. I know what's in it, I know how important she is for you. What I don't know is what he wants from her; she knows nothing, she is nothing to him. But it was the only thing he took out from the laboratory. He never let it of his hand, he was holding it as if it was the most valuable thing in the whole universe. I have no idea what you are planning on doing, but I felt it my obligation to let you know about it. From all four of us, I was the one that chose you. I was the one that pushed to put you as head, and you have proven me right. You made me proud and you help me in ways you can never understand. I have no kids, I spent my whole life chasing politics and money, and I succeeded. What I failed to do was to make a family. Somehow, I feel you are as my own son, the son I never had and always dreamed of. Take care, my son, and I wish one day in the future we can talk again."

Dr Stan: "Don't close yet, please. Tell me who you are, I need to know. If he finds you, he will kill you and I will never know. Please, don't let me wonder, there is no point in hiding anymore."

Man on the phone: "If I die, then it means that all four of us are dead. I will give you a hint, then - I will be the American. Take care."

The line closes. Dr Stan knew this day would come. He knew it the very first time he heard that One had escaped. Knowing is one thing, being prepared another, and being ready a totally different thing. He knew, he thought he was prepared, but he was not ready. He never ever thought this would include Nicky. He was ready at any time to die, he didn't really care; he had no kids, his parents died years ago, he had no family, he only had Nicky. He broke her heart and he had put his own in the freezer, in order to get her far away from him, away from any possible danger. He did all of that for nothing. She was in grave danger and he had no way of protecting her. Suddenly, he remembered Nova. He tried to call him numerous times but his phone was off. In his desperation, he started shouting like crazy, "Nova, I know you can hear me, I know you are aware of everything. Help me, Nova! Nova! Please, she is all I have!" Then he burst in tears. His heart was out of the freezer and it was bleeding. He made his decision; he was going to her. She had family now, two kids and a loving husband. He never lost track of her; he knew everything about her life. He watched her from the shadows like a hungry man looks at other people eating. He managed to stay out of her life completely. He was satisfied that she was okay and she got the life she deserved. He took the phone. He tried to call her but she wouldn't respond. He then called her house. No response, either. He called her husband, again silence. He took a gun he had in the house and ran to his car. He knew where she lived, she was only fifteen minutes away. While he was driving, he kept shouting for Nova. He kept trying to call her and Nova, but nothing, nobody answered. Suddenly, his attention went onto the radio. He hadn't even noticed it was open.

Breaking news: minutes before, the private jet of Donald Marcus exploded in mid-air a few seconds after it left the airport. Rescue units are in the area looking for survivors, but the chances of finding anyone alive are unrealistic. No official comments made yet by the white house. We will come back to you as soon as we have more on the story. Donald was the minister of defence. Dr Stan then realised that the voice he heard on the phone before belonged to him. He was the person known to him as Voice 1. One made this, he continued his senseless violence, he wasn't going to stop. While he was thinking of the dead minister and the other three voices, he realises that if One was in that area, he couldn't be at Nicky's place. He felt a bit more relaxed; he believed he had time to save her. All he had to do was to be there before him. He would take her and her family and go to that room with lead, the one where they treated Nova before. There, he would never find them. All would be good, all he had to do was be faster than him. Yes, that is all there is to it, just be faster. After a couple of minutes of crazy driving, he was there. He was outside the house he thought he would never, ever enter. But there he was, in front of the door. He wrang the door bell, his heart was beating like crazy. Her car was there, she was there, it was quiet, lights inside, and nothing to even suggest something was wrong. Suddenly, the door opened, but nobody was behind it. His hope just died and his fears came back to life. The atmosphere there was heavy, you could hardly breathe. He knew he was there; he was afraid of what would follow. He didn't give a shit about his life, he feared that Nicky's heart would break again, he feared that she would again lose someone she loved - or even worse, that she would lose her life. Having these dark thoughts running in his mind, he kept moving. He reached the living room; there she was, sitting at the sofa, next to two kids, her kids. One son, six years old, and a daughter, four years old. They both looked like her, and all three of them looked terrified. Nicky looked at him; she couldn't say a word, she was too scared to talk. She couldn't control the muscles of her body, and she was shacking uncontrollably. She was hugging her two kids who seemed lost and scared. He turned his head to the other side of the living room. There he was; tall, masculine, lean, with his characteristic white hair and red eyes. He then noticed something of a shadow next to him. It was not his shadow, though, he recognised what it was. He saw it before but only on pictures. That was what remained of Nicky's husband, that was what was left of the kids' father. He killed him in front of them. He had no feelings, no remorse, no mercy, just a cause. But what was his cause? Why hasn't he killed them, why was he waiting for Dr Stan? He wanted to kill him? He could do it, right there right then, all he had to do was think about it and he'd be a shadow. Dr Stan turned and looked at him in the eyes. He never saw a person with red eyes before. They looked like lava; they felt so warm, they felt so inviting, he couldn't explain it, but he was feeling calm. He thought that it was worth a shot to try and talk to him. He tried to open his mouth when suddenly he heard a noise. It was a soft noise, it only lasted for a moment, but that moment was enough. That moment was the decisive moment, the moment that changed everything, that changed him. He turned, he looked at the sofa, he saw three black shadows where they had been sitting. His legs abandoned him, he was on his knees crying uncontrollably, his mind couldn't process what had just happened. Why? For what cause? Why not me, why them? He took his gun and turned it to his head; he pulled the trigger. He felt the barrel of the gun pushing him, but nothing. He opened his eyes. The gun was not in his hands anymore, it was nowhere to be found. He looked One in the eyes, and asked him, why? You owe me at least that much. Why? One went to him, touched his head and told him, "One day, you will have your answer." He then left from the main door that he entered by. Dr Stan went on the couch, laid down on the shadows, crawled, and took the embryonic position. He wasn't able to cry anymore, he didn't know how to react. He hoped this was just a dream, and when he woke up, everything would be as it was back then, back when he was a boring professor at a boring university. He spent three days on that couch. He only moved from it to go and get more alcohol from the bar. He was sleeping most of the time, he dreamed his previous life, he dreamed that he was in a nightmare with superhumans and dead kids, he dreamed he was dreaming. On the third day, a presence woke him. He felt it, it was similar to that of Nova and One; but this was different, this was stronger, more composed, calm and peaceful. He opened his eyes, and saw a man sitting on the chair that was across the living room. He was wearing something like a tight black jumpsuit. His body looked similar to Nova; same structure, hight, composure, but he had dark black hair and purple eyes. He knew he was one of them, but how? Supposedly, only those two existed. How the fuck had this guy skipped their radar? Why is he here? What does he want? Haven't they had enough?

Dr Stan: "I know what you are. I don't know who you are and I don't give a shit. If you are here to kill me, do it, you will be doing me a favour. I've had enough with this life, time to move on to the next one."

Astra: "You don't know what I am, but you will find out. My name is Astra. Now you know and you will give a shit. I am not here to kill you, I am here to resurrect you, and yes, I agree it's time for you to move on to the next life. I am having this verbal conversation with you because at this point, this is the best way for you to understand me, anything else will be too much for you now. In a few minutes I will show you everything, and then you will not have to ask any more questions, as there will be no reason for them."

Dr Stan: "What the fuck do you mean by 'everything'?"
Astra: "Everything."

With one move, Astra was in front of him. He touched him and the Doctor lost consciousness. He was where Nova had been before when he entered Captain's mind. He saw the very same things; he saw the story of existence, the way Earth came to be, our creations. He also saw the two insistences, the internal mothers. He now knew where Nova and One came from, he knew more for them than they knew for themselves. Now he found himself in the Nevada desert. He saw Nova; he was practising, he was naked from the middle and up, and he was standing still looking east. Suddenly, the earth shook, a strange buzz, and then out of nowhere, a huge piece of metal came out of the earth. It must have been buried miles below. It was as big as a passenger plane. It hovered up in the sky at about fifty feet above the ground, then Nova looked at it and it just melted. It transformed into melted iron, then as it was about to hit the ground, about one metre from it, it became solid again. This time it had taken the shape of a sphere. At that moment, the noise of Nova's phone broke the silence. He lost his attention and the sphere became lava again. Dr Stan knew that he was the only one who had his number, he knew he was witnessing the moments when he was desperate and shouted at him. Nova grabbed his head with his two hands and dropped on his knees. He put out a scream and shouted, "Let me concentrate! I can't help you. Get out of my mind, shut up." He heard him; he knew he cried for his help, he felt his desperation and he did nothing, he just ignored him. For what, to train? He could have saved them, or at least tried. If he was there, then his fucking brother would have had what he wanted from him and he would have let them be. He was equally responsible; no, he was worse. Supposedly he was his friend. How could he do that? The journey continued; he now was with One. He was in a cave, just sitting there doing nothing. It was like he was waiting time to pass, like he was supposed to be out of the picture. With a sudden move, One was up, and he was looking at him, but how? He looked at him and smiled. Then Dr Stan heard a voice inside his head; it was One's voice, he recognized it, but his lips weren't moving. It was obvious that they were somehow connected now. The voice said only a single word: "YES."

Dr Stan opened his eyes. He was in a strange room. It was a

big room, white, everything in it white. In that room it was that man - what was his name? Oh yes, Astra, what a strange name. He heard Astra's voice inside his head.

Astra: "You've been out for eight days, that's how long it took for you to be reborn. You are on my ship, or as you humans say, my spaceship. On the corner of the ground, you will find one uniform. It will fit your body better than the dirty suit you are wearing. It will enhance your power and help you control it. You will also find a helmet. Wear it for as long as you are near them, it will block them from entering your mind. You are now connected to our conciseness; you are almost one of us. It will take some time for you to sync, and so some knowledge and powers will come to you later on. It doesn't have a particular time line, usually it takes some sort of emotional shock to awake everything. You will need some time to get used to what you have become. You are my guest here but you cannot leave unless and when I say so, and only when you are ready. If you leave now, you and the whole planet are doomed."

Dr Stan went to the corner of the room, saw a black uniform, the same Astra was wearing, and he also saw a black helmet. It resembled an old Viking helmet; it had two horns coming out of it. He took off his clothes, he stayed put for a while, he saw his naked body, and got shocked, how could this happen in just eight days? He grew; he was bigger, leaner, he looked like them. He finally put on his new clothes and his helmet, and he felt the difference, he felt his muscles pumping oxygen. He felt concentrated, focused. It was like seeing for the very first time. He was reborn, he felt invisible, powerful, superior. Astra watched him getting dressed when he decided to talk to him.

Astra: "Now, about the uniform; that technology was used

against us by the Molicours, a race that is almost identical to humans. When we conquered them, we found out ways to adjust it to our own specs and connect it to our DNA. It is actually made of living organisms. They can heal and absorb most of the damage you may take. They multiply themselves and they are connected by your skin to your brain. They enhance your senses and you will have a 360-degree view. They will help you with the task you are given. The helmet; that we couldn't reproduce. Its technology is a mystery even for us. The design is barbaric, but we kept all the helmets at their original state. Changing anything on them will make them useless. They were invented and used against us by a far superior form of life than us, the Superlorks. They no longer exist; they were a race of proud warriors. Their physical strength unlike anything we ever encountered. The war with them lasted longer than any other. In the beginning we managed to win most of the battles using our psychic powers and corrupting their brains, but on one battle they came wearing those helmets - it was a massacre. The few of us left alive retreated and regrouped. We waited for years until new-borns grew enough, and we calculated every possible strategy so we can defeat them. The outcome was always the same. We knew if we attacked again, they would made us extinct. Until one day, we found their weakness; they had feelings, they had the curse of caring. A selected group of us entered their nursery and took all their infants. They came to negotiate. The terms were simple: deliver all of their helmets and they will live. As I told you, none of them exist anymore... that was our darkest hour. We spared not even the infants, although there is a rumour that some of the infants were spared and live in exile, but that was never proven. What you need to know is that, although forbitten and punished by death, some of us found ways of hiding things from the consciousness, so be aware and never act like you know everything. What you see and what you know is not always what it is, but when the time comes and you are sync, then you will acquire knowledge beyond any possible expectations."

Dr Stan: "I feel very strange, I cannot describe it. I don't think I can control all I now have, but I will try. I've seen the truth, I know the truth, I know what to do and I will do what needs to be done."

Astra: "Eliminate them before they destroy Earth. We need Earth, it is the nursery for a greater civilisation than ours, it is our legacy, humans need time to grow before they are allowed to reach their heartache. Those two are abominations, they were never supposed to happen, humanity needs to remain as pure as possible. That was the line that was not to be passed. Now you will fix it. You will fix it, and then you have two choices: come with us away from this solar system, join our quest for learning and maintaining balance in the universe, or end yourself and let humanity be." Dr Stan didn't reply. He blocked any thoughts and emotions and just moved on and looked out of the only window that was there. It was so peaceful, so surrealistic. A few days ago, he was in a car with his superhuman friend drinking scotch and now he was a superhuman in a spaceship looking at deep space, wearing a ridiculous helmet with horns. The strangest thing of all was that it didn't feel strange at all.

Years have passed since that day. Everything back on earth looked the same. The incident at the psychiatric institute at Boston was classified as a terrorist attack. Supposedly the terrorist used chemical weapons and the area stayed off limits by the military until every single piece of evidence disappeared. The project division was no more. Nobody ever heard of the four men who controlled the whole project. Everyone involved directly in the project was dead, everyone except Dr Lee. You see the day of the intrusions she decided not to hide in the freezer or any of the offices. She opened the amniotic reservoir and entered inside, her instinct drove her there. The whole incident only lasted a few seconds. One's senses were obviously blocked by the fluid, there was no other logical explanation, otherwise he would have killed her, no reason not to. When he was finally out and she decided to exit the tank, she witnessed something extraordinary; without a sparkle, without any flammable liquid and without a warning, fire exploded from thin air. It was such a brutal and sudden explosion that pushed her violently back into the reservoir. She woke up a few minutes later and found herself floating in the amniotic. The fire only lasted for a few seconds but it was enough to leave almost nothing behind it. When she was interviewed about the incident, she claimed to remembered nothing. She said that all that she remembered was a big bang and then just silence. That day she went home, opened a bottle of wine and then a second one, she couldn't sleep. She stayed on her couch until morning. When the first dawn lights hit her face, she decided to stand up. She walked outside of the house, went in the back, and opened another door that led to the basement. She walked down the steps, one by one, but every step was taken in a slower pace than the previous, she wasn't sure if she took the correct decision. She was finally down. She turned the lights on. It was her personal laboratory, her handwritten notes and everything else kept in secrecy from the project team, was hidden there. Of course, it was prohibited to keep any notes for herself but she did. She was smart enough to know not to put them on a PC, as those could be easily accessed either by one of them or the government, or anyone with adequate knowledge. She kept everything, years of work, years of study, every single detail. She felt she was in danger, she was the only survivor and it was impossible to complete the total coverup with her alive. It was either the black ops or One who would come for her first. She took her notes and put them in a briefcase. She then opened a hatch on the floor. It was a fridge. Inside was various fluids in bottles with handwritten notes on them. She put them in a handbag with enough ice and left the house, she was going to disappear. The black ops did come to the house. Their orders were clear: eliminate her and make it look like a suicide. Her laboratory was discovered as well as the empty fridge on the ground. The house was burned to the ground and everything left in that laboratory was taken and kept for further study.

One had been in his cave for years now, undetected, untouched. His body had no pulse and his brain was deactivated, he was in a position known as Lotus position, which is a cross-legged sitting meditation pose from ancient India, in which each foot is placed on the opposite thigh. He was in some sort of hibernation, he resembled a well-preserved mummy, when finally, on one day like any other, he opened his red eyes. Blood started pumping through his veins, his brain activity came back and his cold body got warmer. He stood up. His beard and hair reached his waste, he was still wearing the same pants but they were full of holes and half eaten by the rats in the cave. He stood still for a couple of minutes until he regained his full capacity, then he slowly walked out of the cave. When he was outside, he turned to look up to the sky, and then east. He smiled as he was heading barefoot down the mountain having east in front of him.

The same time he got out of that cave, a big earthquake

happened in the Nevada desert. Nova sensed his awakening. He was different now. He had lived alone for years, just training, meditating, and learning how to use his powers. The awakening of his brother shocked his senses and unwillingly made him move the ground, although he practiced so hard and was so focused, he had yet mastered and controlled everything. He hadn't learned to control his emotions to perfection. The same signals travelled to the other side of the universe. Dr Stan felt the awakening of the man who killed everything he ever cared about. He managed to master his emotions and learned how to control his rage, he was perfect. He was calm and prepared for what was coming. He also felt Nova's vibes. He understood that he failed to control his powers but he felt his reserves. He was strong, stronger than he ever thought he'd be, but he had no control, and power without control was weakness. Astra was no longer with him. He left him years ago to pursue his quest. Astra knew that the Doctor had perfected and mastered his potentials, and so he left him to fulfil his destiny, his task. He was going to come later to either take him with him, or make sure he would be no more.

Nova teleported himself to Las Vegas; that was one of the many abilities he discovered hidden within him. He was now outside the MGM Grand. He entered and walked to the reception. He looked like a homeless man; he had a long, black, thick beard, his hair hadn't seen a comb for ages and reached his elbows, he was wearing some old torn up grey linen pants and a shirt which at some point should have been white, he had no shoes, and he was covered in desert sand. The receptionist looked at him, she was both surprised and experienced, she turned and looked at the also surprised and experienced security guard, who was only a few feet away. He came there and stood next to Nova, he saw this happening numerous times during the years, crazy and homeless people been there before, but something seemed different with the man he had in front of him now.

Nova: "I would like the presidential suite, please."

Receptionist: "Sir, I think that the prices may be a little out of your budget. Maybe you would like to try one of the city models. Frank can give you directions on your way out."

Nova then gave her a gold credit card; not gold in colour, but made of gold. She never saw such a card and she thought it must be fake.

Receptionist: "Sir, please don't make me feel bad. We kindly request you to step out. We will even call you a cab."

Nova: "Humour me and try to make a payment for a four day stay."

The girl, in order to get him out of there, and without causing a scene, acted as she was told. She was surprised to see that the card came through. She looked at this man, and this time she saw an attractive, well-built man and not a beggar, somehow that gold card made him more interesting and mysterious, and somehow suddenly he got the most mesmerizing blue eyes she ever saw.

Receptionist: "My apologies, sir, but you must admit that your looks right now don't really back up your attempt. Your room will be ready in a few minutes."

Nova: "Well, I couldn't agree more. Please, make a deposit of one hundred thousand dollars to my room's account with that card. The ten thousand is yours. Also, please send somebody to take my measurements in my room. I think I need a new suit and shoes. Also, I would like to have spaghetti with lobster. I would also like three bottles of Louis Roederer Cristal Gold

Medalion Orfevres Limited Edition Brut, a box of Cohiba Spectre, and I would like to see you when you are through with your shift."

The girl laughed, again did as she was told, and she checked her watch. She needed one more hour to finish her shift, but that was ok, he needed a good shower first, and she wasn't interested on helping him on that. Suddenly an idea came to her mind, and she felt comfortable of executing it, she took the liberty to order him a watch. She chose a black leather IWC and gave instructions for it to be handed to him with the champagne. Nova was now in his room, it's been years since the last time he had the luxury of a bed and a shower. He went into the bathroom, stayed in the bath for half an hour, washed his hair, shaved, freshened up and opened one of the bottles. He never accepted anyone opening his bottles, it was something that brought him happiness, the sound of the cork popping has something magical, it was part of the whole process. He was totally aware of what was coming, but right now he cared more about the receptionist than anything else.

Meanwhile, Dr Stan's spaceship was heading to Earth. He was calm and ready to encounter both his nemesis and his former friend. The only thing he was sure about was that he wanted to start from One; he was number one, after all... The fight was doubtful, it was anyone's game, but at the end, only one of them would live to tell the story. Dr Stan was wearing the black tight uniform and had his helmet next to him. It didn't matter how powerful he was; if any of them entered his mind, then the balances would change. He was created; they were born like that. It was their battleground and he would lose. He had more life experience than them, he was hurt the most, he had memories, griefs, moments of joy, of regret. He was assailable there. He mastered his emotions, he could hide everything, but he couldn't make them disappear. What made him human was his biggest vulnerability now, but he had his helmet for that. They could not get in. Travelling back to Earth after so many years... It was the first time that he actually thought about what may have changed after all these years. How did they cover up the destruction that One left behind him? Or do people know about the existence of them? No, it was impossible. G.O.D programs were the biggest secret since the time of the pyramids. They found a way, they always do. Who is in charge now? Does the G.O.D project even exist? Everybody was dead. As far as he knew, the sponsors were dead as well, and the project's subject was in Nevada playing superman, so yes, the project was done for. How about Nicky's family? do they even know she is dead? There was no body to be buried. It would be easier to cover up the whole thing with her, any story goes. She took the kids and her husband and disappeared. She drowned during a boat trip. She was in an airplane crash, whatever. It didn't matter; all that mattered was that she and her two kids died in front of him. One killed them, and for some reason he wanted him to witness it, but why? This was the question that troubled him, this was what he was thinking all the time, during his training, his rest time, his breathing time. Even mediation couldn't help him - this was his burden. He wanted to get the reason out of One's lips right before he died in his hands. This answer was all that mattered, and this was the reason he willingly accepted everything that Astra offered him. If he got that answer, then it wouldn't matter if he lived or died. That thought kept him company all the way until Earth's atmosphere. When he reached it, he opened a hatch and jumped out of the spaceship. He knew that the presence of a spaceship was forbitten. People on Earth should never learn they exist, they should never learn they were made in the image and likeness of them. It was better to believe in grey and green little persons, because that was more acceptable than the actual truth. He kept gliding down the atmosphere. When he reached an altitude of about two thousand feet, he reduced his speed and gained control over gravity. He was hovering while slowly descending, and he landed in a remote area near California. His descent there was not by luck; he felt One's presence nearby. He couldn't exactly pin-point it but he wasn't far away. Although Dr Stan had the uniform, the helmet, and his relatively new powers, he knew that he would be an equal and not a superior opponent for One. It was about 03:00, dark and hot, and nobody was around. He was alone, he was back on Earth after so long. He missed the atmosphere; the air, the gravity, the sounds. He now realised how much he missed home. He never actually thought about it before. He was so focused on his training and so tortured by that question that he almost forgot he was human. He sat down on the ground, took off his helmet, and just looked around; looked at the sky, the stars, the moon. He then noticed what was around him; the trees, the vegetation, the city lights. He stayed there until the morning. For a moment, he forgot about everything. One, Nova, her, the kids, Astra. He just existed, for a short moment that seemed to have lasted for an eternity, but that eternity wasn't enough. It was dawn when he felt it; he felt One trying to sneak into his head. He put the helmet on and stood up. He couldn't understand where he was. One was experienced and confident in his powers. He knew how to hide his aura, his existence, he was almost invisible from Dr Stan. At that point, the Doctor understood that One wanted to be found, otherwise he could have used this ability when he woke up and there would be no way, or at least no easy way, to get his stigma. Was this a trap? Had he led him to a trap? Again, it made no sense. If he wanted him dead, he could have done so years ago. He had his chance, but he let him live. Why? Again, that fucking word, why? He was going to find out one way or the other, even if it killed him. It just didn't matter anymore.

Dr Stan: "I know you don't like to use your voice, but let's keep it as basic as we can. You can't get in my mind to do our conversation there. I have a lot of questions for you, but I'd prefer to have you half-dead first and then ask them."

One: "Thank you for being on time. And thank you for finding me, I couldn't find you. You see, that helmet you have on your head actually works."

One appeared in the background, walking towards Dr Stan. He was wearing his old and torn pair of pants and he was half-naked, no shoes at all. His eyes were glowing. He was already in battle mode. This was the first time he knew he would face an equal opponent. He was excited about that. The uncertainty of the outcome had filled his existence.

One: "I promise you one thing: whatever the outcome is, at the end I will answer it. I will answer your question."

Dr Stan: "Enough talking. Now you die."

What I am about to describe happened in the context of a few seconds. A normal observer could only see the outcome and not what actually happened before. The speed that unfolded was such that not even the powers of nature could control anything there. Dr Stan ran to One. He grabbed him by the neck with one hand, put him up and pushed him to the ground with such a force that the ground below retreated and a small shell hole created. Then as he was still holding him by the neck, and holding his head on the ground, he started running, rubbing his face on the ground. This had left a line on the ground. He stopped and once again, One was up in the air while Dr. Stan was holding his neck. He threw him with all his force and he only stopped several metres away after cutting down two trees with his body. One was up on his feet. He was bleeding from his nose and ears, his half-naked body was covered in dirt and blood. He looked at Dr Stan and smiled. Then, without a warning and without making any noise, the terms turned. He was holding the Doctor by the neck.

One: "You did well. You would be a great ally to me. We could do greatness together. But sadly for you, I don't need any ally. What I need, you brought. Now let's finish this."

He started choking him with one hand while punching him all over with the other. His punches were so strong that his uniform started changing colours. From black it became blue, then yellow, green, and finally red. Although it was designed to absorb everything and heal the owner's wounds, it couldn't offer much against One's fierce attack. Dr Stan tried to control his breathing while he punched back with everything he had. He could see that his punches inflicted damage to One's body, he saw his body bruise and bleed, but he also saw that his facial expression was still the same; it was like he trained himself not to feel pain. A few moments before he lost consciousness, something happened. It was like a new ability was downloaded into him. All of a sudden, he found himself metres away from One; he had teleported. He saw One with one hand yet up in the air like he was still holding him. This was what Astra meant when he said it would take time and maybe emotional stress to wake up some of his potentials. He now had the power to teleport. His uniform changed colours again, from red to green, from green to yellow, then blue and finally back to black, it had healed itself. He actually felt his body healing and his power reinstated.

One: "Bravo, that's a smart trick. I haven't figured that out, yet. Actually, there is a lot I need to learn, and I will. You see, I am not connected to that collectiveness you are connected to. I am an outcast, an abomination, I am not worthy of them. That's what they think and that's what they most likely have told you. I cannot get into your mind, but my mind works differently than yours and theirs. I can see things you cannot, I can see them using you to kill me. They are afraid of me, they know I am born and raised for combat, that I am influenced and programmed to kill and predict strategies. They don't want me dead because I am a danger to Earth; they want me dead because I am a danger to them. They sent you as a guinea pig, you are here so they can study me, so they can find ways to kill me. They think they have put you in this position you are. I have news for you, news you cannot forward to them, unless you want to take off your helmet. I've put you here. I made your destiny, I needed you for something, I created the circumstances, I am the one who made the checkmate, not them. I will win this battle and then the war."

Dr Stan: "I don't give a shit about any of that, all I care about is your death. I need it in order for me to continue living, or at least to die in peace."

Dr Stan raised his hands up in the air. Between the space of his palms, you could now see a white bright light. As the moments passed, that light got brighter and thicker. He had actually created and gathered all the static electricity in the area, and when all of it was in his hands, he threw it at him. One did not expect that; he could control some elements but not electricity. He was sure that the Doctor would be familiar and in some control of some elements, but not electricity, and not to that level. The electric bolt hit his body. He felt his insides boiling; he could smell his flesh burning. That was pain, he thought, that was real pain, everything else before that was a joke. Everything could be controlled and absorbed one way or the other, even the bruises from before were healed, but this? This was something else, another level of pain, another level of agony. It was then that he actually felt that he could not fulfil his destiny, his duty. He knew he was near extinction. As suddenly as it started, suddenly it finished. All the electricity in the area was done for. You see, they were outside of the city - no houses, no buildings, no man-made electricity available, only what nature could produce. That gave One a fighting chance. His body immediately initiated the self-healing process but he knew he didn't have enough time to regain his powers. If he stayed there, he would die. All that the Doctor had to do was to make his next move, which would be a certain fatal one. One stood up. He felt he had the capability to fly. He never felt that before and he never even attempted such a thing. He looked up to the sky, the same time that Dr Stan was running towards him. He knelt, and with one push of his legs, he was kilometres up in the sky. He could fly. Dr Stan didn't possess that capability, or hadn't figured out how to do it yet. He stayed on the ground looking up to the sky. Although his eyesight was far superior to any being on the planet, he could not locate One. He was far gone.

One was already far away. He was hurting, bleeding, his insides were burned. A normal human, actually any normal living organism, should have been dead long before. He was back in his cave, he was totally naked, the few clothes he had on him were evaporated and burned. He laid on the ground. He was more confused than anything else; he thought he had the perfect strategy, he thought he had everything under control, he believed that he would win the fight, get what he needed and then finalize his plan. He planned everything. They all thought he was inactive all these years in the tank, but just as his brother, he was not. He was aware of everything that was happening around him. While in the amniotic tank, he was conscious. He had no choice but to be subjected to all the experiments, all the training and tactics, all the information that was downloaded into his brain. He wasn't strong enough before and he had no reason to get out of there. He waited for his brother's awakening. That was the correct moment, that was the first step of his plan. He then knew that the others would find a way to intervene, and he knew they were not allowed an active part in this. He also knew that they would use somebody else to do their dirty work. He studied all possible candidates and he carefully eliminated every single one of them - or so he thought. He only left Dr Stan alive because he thought that his thirst for revenge would make him vulnerable. He needed the equipment that he would be given, he needed it so he could move on to the next step. The next step would be confronting his brother and absorbing his powers. He needed all that so he could end what he started. But right now, he needed a new plan to get the Doctor's gifts. He should get stronger and work smarter. He was not in control anymore; he was the pray and the Doctor was the hunter. But first thing's first, he needed to recover and regain all that was lost. He decided to stay in that cave until full recovery with the hope that he would not be spotted. In order to do that, he shut down all of his powers and left only what was necessary to heal himself. If he blocked that ability too, he would be dead in a heartbeat.

Back in Vegas, Nova was sitting out on his suite balcony. He felt the battle, he felt the enormous power release, and he felt his brother hurting. He couldn't locate the source of the power that did this to his brother - the helmet blocked everything. He remembered what he was told when deep in Captain's brain. He was sure that one of them decided to intervene, that was what must have happened. One or more of them was already there, and if they found One, they would find him. He was next. He couldn't feel his brother anymore. He was either dead or somewhere recovering. It seemed that he had more than just One to worry about. He decided to leave Vegas; if something started there, the casualties would be enormous. He needed to go back to the desert and wait for him or them to find him. He felt confident in himself. 'Let them come, I am prepared, I am at my peak, whatever happens, happens. In the end, maybe they are right; we should never be, but okay, it is what it is and I am ready for any outcome. I just hope that Dr Stan is doing well. I lost his stigma a long time ago, but somehow, I know he is alive,' he thought to himself. He called the reception and ordered two large bags. He also ordered twelve bottles of wine, four bottles of single malts, two boxes of cigars, and a lot of water. And of course, he ordered a rental car, to carry everything. He packed everything and got down to the reception. On duty was the receptionist he saw when he first went there. He was wearing a black suit with a black shirt, shoes, and the IWC she ordered for him.

Receptionist: "I thought you would stay for at least a week."

Nova: "Yeah, you see, something happened at the office and I must leave immediately. But I would like to get your number."

She gave him a piece of paper with her number on it. He wasn't planning on calling her or seeing her again, but asking her phone was the easiest way out of it. They said goodbye and he went in the car. Of course, he could teleport himself, but he couldn't take with him anything more than just his clothes. It was impossible to take all the alcohol and everything else with him, so he decided to rent a car and drive back to the desert. He finally reached his destination in the early morning, at dawn. There was the car he took from Dr Stan years ago. It was useless, eaten by sand and sun. He used to use it as a bed during his training. For food and water, he learned to use his powers. Animals came to him and just died in front of him so he could eat them. Water was just created out of the humidity of night. Of course, he could not create fine wine, champagne, cigars and everything else he brought with him. His plan was to wait there until they came for him. That was the place of his big battle, the place he would face his enemies, the appropriate and selected battleground. He exited the rental car and walked near Dr Stan's car to take some of the stuff there. He preferred that as a bed instead of the old rental one. When he reached the car, he noticed a man sitting at the driver's seat. He was surprised; normally he should have felt his presence and read his mind, especially in such a close ratio. He cautiously walked up to the passenger's window. He took a look inside. He couldn't see the man's face as he was looking straight and almost his whole face was covered by a strange looking helmet with two horns. He noticed that he was wearing a black uniform, similar to the one the others were wearing. He thought that he was one of them, he was the one who managed to hurt his brother. As he was thinking of how to react, a known voice came out of the man's mouth.

Dr Stan: "I thought you would take more care of my car. I used to love this car. I have a lot of good memories in here. But I am not surprised. I know now what I didn't know then. You only care for yourself; nobody and nothing else matters for you. I guess I must take some blame on that."

Nova: "I didn't know if you were alive or dead, but something inside me reassured me that you are yet alive and well, despite the lack of knowledge of your whereabouts. I couldn't reach you, I couldn't locate your stigma, but I was sure you were alive. I am so happy to see you."

Dr Stan: "Nova, I am not here to discuss old times with you, I am here to kill you. Although it would be good to have some good old single malt and a Cohiba before that."

Nova: "Well, I know how stubborn you are and I am not going to try and change your mind. But yes, scotch and cigars sound great."

The two men sat there for hours, and the first bottle became the second, and the second, third. They discussed everything except what happened after their last time together. That was a taboo, at least for now. They both felt happy they were together again. They didn't want that moment to end. At that moment, everything seemed simple; just two friends in the Nevada desert drinking and laughing. All that mattered was the moment they shared, at the end of the day. What is life if not shared moments?

Nova: "Did you voluntarily put that on your head, or is it some kind of lost bet? A punishment? Or you are trying to kill me with your bad taste in hats?"

Dr Stan: "I know everything that you do. I actually know more. You see, I was taken by them. I was given powers, trained, I was getting prepared for you and your brother. I am here to kill both of you, and in order to do so, I needed something to protect my mind. Well, that something is this stupid looking helmet."

Nova: "You didn't even think of making some changes to that? I mean, you look like a goat on steroids. At least cut the horns."

Dr Stan: "My dear old friend, it's getting late. Your brother must be regaining his powers and studying ways to defeat me. I must find him before he is fully regenerated, so I am afraid we've already had all the time we could spare. I do not possess all the psychic abilities you and your brother have, although some I have. I am only a human, after all; but as you will see, all that matters in this fight is brute strength. I am sure that you noticed that you can't get in my mind, as this helmet blocks you from entering my mind."

Nova: "But it doesn't block you from entering mine, yes?"

Dr Stan: "I have already been in your mind. No surprises there…"

Nova: "My good friend. You went as far as I allowed you. You see, I have evolved, in every possible way. Some things I can hide, even from you - actually, from everybody. You want to take a look there before you kill me?"

Dr Stan: "I am very curious to see what you've been hiding, my old friend."

He put his hand on Nova's head and closed his eyes. He knew he was more vulnerable now, but he also knew that Nova wouldn't use a cheap trick like that. It was true, he found a whole new world of memories and thoughts inside his mind. He was indeed able to hide parts of his mind. He saw his time at the desert, the endless hours of training, he felt the despair, he felt his disparity, he felt his doubts. He wasn't as arrogant as he thought he was, he was actually more a human than most of the humans he knew. He had all the normal feelings anyone would have had in his position. Now he was at the point that he was calling for him, desperate for help, but this time he was seeing things through Nova's eyes. He was hearing his own voice calling him, he saw him dropping to his knees and crying, repeating, "I am not ready yet, I am not ready yet." Dr Stan was sure that he would go on and see something else, maybe some more training, drinking, or whatever. Instead of that, he saw him standing outside Nicky's house. He teleported himself, he saw through his eyes watching from the window, the insides of the house. Somehow, One wasn't able to discover him - he was like a ghost. What happened next shocked him. He couldn't believe what had happened. How could he not see that, how could he not feel them? He saw Nova entering the house, going into the living room where everyone was. He saw himself standing still. Nova had managed to freeze or slow time. He went, took her and the two kids, got some ashes from the ground - the ones that had been left from her husband - and put them on the couch. He then went and touched his brother on the forehead and left. He took with him Nicky and her kids. They were alive, he took care of them, he listened, he acted, he cared, he risked and he delivered. He felt a big shock passing through his body as he opened his eyes. Nova's brain pushed him out. He started crying. He couldn't stop, he couldn't control it. He was sure that all of his emotions were under his total control - again, he was wrong.

Nova: "They are safe, but I cannot allow you to find out their whereabouts. I don't know what they've done to you. I don't know what they want from you and all I know is that they will be safer like that, at least for now. As for my brother, that day he saw what I implanted in his mind, what I needed him to see. I am so sorry I haven't taken you with me or haven't told you the truth, but it was the only safe way for this to work. It's you who he wanted; he needed you alive for some reason. I knew that the moment I touched him. As for the reason, I have no idea. He managed to lock parts of his brain, as well."

Dr Stan: "Thank you, thank you, and sorry I ever doubted you. I should have known better."

Nova: "Don't mention it. You will take me out for dinner at a very expensive restaurant and you will be a gentleman. That should suffice."

Both men laughed and continued drinking for a while. Suddenly, they both stopped and looked at the sky. They felt an enormous and heavy vibe in the air; they knew something was wrong. They stood up and waited for whatever was to appear. They felt its hostility, they knew it was coming for them. Something hit the ground, something that created a big earthquake in the surrounding area. Dust was blocking the morning sun, as well as the direct view. The dust had begun to back off, and they could now see the silhouette of a man. Dr Stan recognised that man - it was Astra. He wasn't wearing his usual black uniform, he was in a red one, and for the first time, he was wearing a helmet similar to his but with three horns. Nova had no idea who the man was, but he could recognise the uniform style and the body structure. He was one of them, one of the others. His aura was different, more powerful than anything he had felt before. He tried to understand what was going on but it was almost impossible as he couldn't get inside his mind. As he was trying to comprehend everything, he felt something, he felt the man intruding his brain - but he was ready for that. He closed his eyes and until he opened them, that man was blocked out.

Astra: "Bravo, number two. I thought you were the weak one - obviously I was wrong. You have my respect. Nobody ever managed to block me out of his mind. I will introduce myself to you. The Doctor already knows my name but not my title. I am Prince Astra, the ruler of all Celians, your creators. Now, let's get down to business. At the end of the day, and as you people say on Earth, time is money. Although I never understood the stupidity of creating such a contraption like money. That is as unnecessary as putting traffic lights on the moon. Doctor, I am so disappointed in you; you almost killed number one without even trying, and there you are, crying like a child. Because of what? Because number two saved three mortal souls? You failed to understand one thing, one very simple thing: humans are temporary, we are forever. I made you one of us, a GOD, as you would say here. And? What have you done with that? You got drunk, you got wasted, you got emotional and in a few minutes, you'll get dead. Tell me, was it worth it? You only had one job, a simple task: control your emotions and kill these two parricides. Now I have to intervene and eliminate all three of you, but I will make sure you will be the hero. You killed them and then killed yourself because you didn't want to leave Earth, your home."

Dr Stan: "You actually think I will go down without a fight? And please, tell me why Nova must die? He has proven he is not a threat, he always kept a low profile and always helped humanity. He is not a threat, contrary to his brother."

Astra: "They are abominations, and they must be eliminated. Humanity is a special project which must stay as virgin as possible, for now. There is no room for them here, they are not to exist."

Nova: "Hey, big guy; just out of curiosity, how about coming with you? Is that safe enough for Earth? I really don't want to fight you, at least not on Earth."

Astra: "Enough talking. You must die. Doctor, this is your last chance. Kill him and live."

Dr Stan: "Can I at least finish my drink before I start fighting you? This is a very expensive scotch, you know. Care to join us?"

Nova: "Don't share our scotch with him, he doesn't deserve it."

Astra: "Enough…"

None of them got prepared for Astra. He was simply in a whole different level. It was like putting a heavy weight champion against a rooky. What are the chances? Without them even seeing him, or even understanding what was going on, they were on the ground. Dr Stan had a big hole through his abdominals and Nova had his left hand broken in two places. They were on the ground, they looked at each other, they were scared and hopeless. It was obvious that the two of them couldn't beat him, they couldn't even scratch him. As they were on the ground, they felt another presence, a familiar one. They looked up and saw One dissenting from the sky. He was totally healed and his aura felt stronger. He was different, stronger, they felt his confidence. He looked at them and smiled. It was like he mocked at them.

One: "Take your time and heal yourselves. When you are healed you will feel stronger. That is because you will be stronger. It seems that every time we face a serious injury and manage to recover from it, we come back stronger, it is in our nature. I guess in your nature too, Doctor, as it seems you are one of us, now."

Astra: "You are all abominations. None of you is us, none of you deserve to breathe, all of you will vanish. You interfere with our plan. We sacrificed everything in order to give our kind a second chance. You are liabilities and you'll be dealt with."

Astra unleashed an attack on One. He raised his punches and aimed at his face. He managed to avoid it and actually, while doing so, he inflicted two blows to Astra's torso. Astra was the prince; he never ever missed a war in his whole life. He was as experienced in chaos as any living being could ever be, but this time, this time he felt pain like never before. This time he was surprised. How can a lower being inflict such a pain to him? If he hadn't had his uniform, he would probably be dead. He studied One and Nova; he was no fool, he knew he was up against two strong opponents, but after studying them, he was sure he would easily prevail. But just in case, and in order not to be directly involved, he decided to use the Doctor. He studied him as well; he studied every single person involved in the G.O.D projects. You see, what got their attention in the forgotten realm of Earth was that explosion in Chernobyl. They recognised that power release as one of their own. But until they reached Earth to investigate, that signal was lost, until the two brothers awoke. Then it was decided that they weren't a big threat and agreed to keep an eye on the whole situation, mostly in order to discover who and why created them. They were not supposed to be, so the source of all needed to be found. But something changed; they got stronger, especially One. That punch was not expected and not supposed to happen. He took some steps back so he could avoid any other attacks from him. He was bleeding from the mouth, and his red uniform became grey - it was almost destroyed. He knew he had to buy some time to heal. Not much, just a few more seconds. But in the meantime, Nova and the Doctor were already half-way healed. They couldn't believe how fast they recovered. The wounds were now closed and they actually felt very good.

One: "What's wrong, my friend? You are wondering where I found this power? You didn't see that coming, did you? I will share a secret with you: we were born and raised on Earth. Here, we are close to the sun and we experience gravity. That is something you people don't have. You travelled the whole existence, never stopped conquering, searching for ways to become stronger, and the irony is that the planet you built in order to have your little experimental colony was the answer you searched for. We take power from the sun, we get stronger by Earth itself, we are a part of this ecosystem. It takes care of us, it provides us with all we need. You? You are only here for a few minutes. Even the ones that set up this whole thing were not able to feel that. That is because the ecosystem was primitive and they spent most of the time in their spaceship. I am telling you all this for three reasons: the first is that you will not stay long enough to benefit from that. The second one is that in order to alert the others, you have to take of that helmet of yours, and third - because you will die here."

Astra knew he had to take this more seriously. He now had three opponents to defeat, and he was at a big disadvantage. He had no choice, he had to do something. He had no option but to unleash his rage mode. He'd never used that before. He knew he had the capability, but he kept it for himself. Going into that mode meant that he would not be able to use his psychic abilities as all of his focus and strength would be carried through his muscles. That is a technique that even humans have, as the fight or flight response. The fight or flight response is an automatic physiological reaction to an event that is perceived as stressful or frightening. The perception of threat activates the sympathetic nervous system and triggers an acute stress response that prepares the body to fight or flee. He chose to fight. He took off his helmet and gave a scream, a scream so loud and so frightening that it moved the earth around him. Pieces of earth were now hovering around him. You could see his muscles double in size, his eyes became larger than usual - actually, all you could see in his eyes was a deep purple colour, no white at all. Around him was a huge red aura, it was visible to the naked eye. He stopped screaming when his transformation was complete. He was a beast, a war beast. He didn't even resemble a human being - he looked like a huge gorilla in a red uniform.

Nova: "I thing we are fucked."

Dr Stan: "What makes you say that? Is it just a feeling, or does that huge crazy-looking alien have something to do with it?"

Before Nova answered, Astra was standing in front of them. The mere size of him was intimidating. He used each of his hands and grabbed them by their necks, he kept them up high, and within a safe distance from his body so they couldn't hit him. They felt the air being drawn out of their bodies. Nova tried to enter Astra's mind. He actually managed to get there, but it was an empty space. In this mode he had no memories, no information; it was just an empty space full of rage and primitive instincts of survival. Dr Stan closed his eyes and took his mind far away from the fact he was being choked to death, put his two hands together, and started gathering electricity from the area. He took the electricity out of the two cars, out of the wind, out of everything that could offer him something. When he felt he had enough, he pushed it directly into Astra's chest. At the same time, One grabbed Astra from behind, and the electric burden was released into Astra's body. His uniform on the area of impact became grey again. Suddenly, he released both men and turned his attention to One. Using one hand, he grabbed him by the face and pushed him to the ground with all his force. One was on the ground, Astra's enormous palm pushing his face down. He was bleeding from the nose and struggled to get a breath. If any of them had been fighting there alone, he would have died in an instance, but all three of them had a chance with him - a small chance, but yet a chance. Nova used his time freezing ability, and everything around him stopped. Within a heartbeat, he managed to inflict more than ten blows to Astra's body and get his brother out of his hands. He could only use that ability for a while. Until the time came back to normal, Nova, the Doctor and One were at a safe distance from Astra. They looked at each other and then all of them looked at Astra, who was looking back at them furiously.

Astra: "You are no match for me, not in this form. You have a choice: to run and fight another day, or die here and now."

One: "We will finish this today. You disturbed my plan, you are the anomaly here, and I am not giving you the choice of fleeing. You will vanish here. You were not supposed to interfere with Earth."

Nova: "Well, brother, about that plan of yours. Don't you think it's about time to tell us about it? After all, the chances are that we die here."

One: "All in good time, my brother. First, we finish here."

This time, they made the first move, and all three attacked

Astra; Nova and One confronted him face to face, as the Doctor tried to create electricity again. He blocked all of their attacks with his hands and managed to hit both brothers in the face. They flew for two metres and fell on the ground, then when the Doctor had a clear view, he released his electricity towards Astra. Then Astra did something that surprised all three of them; he put his hands in front of him and caught the electric ball that was supposed to hit him, and he kept his hands up until the ball was absorbed by him, absorbed into his hands. His eyes started sparkling. He used that electric charge as a power cell. He was stronger now, they could feel it; he was adjusting, learning. He was evolving.

Dr Stan: "Well that went we-"

Before he could finish his sentence, he received a blow from Astra to his stomach. His uniform became directly red. His uniform died; he couldn't fell it anymore. He felt naked and unprotected. Astra smiled in Dr Stan's face, then he released another punch, this time directly to the left of his chest. Dr Stan's heart lost its beat. He felt dizzy, he took a step back, looked behind him and saw Nova on the ground. He smiled and managed to say a word, only one word: "sorry". He was on the ground. They couldn't feel his vitals; his heart had stopped - he was dead. Nova couldn't believe that he had lost his friend for the second time, and this time was for good. He was on his feet, he looked at Astra; he was angry, furious, determined. He was going to take revenge for his friend.

Nova: "Let me take his body somewhere safe; respect at least that, and then we will continue this. That's a promise."

Astra moved his head in a positive way. Nova took his friend in his hands while moving away from everything, and went to put his friend in his old car. He looked at him, he took his helmet off and put it next to him, took one bottle of scotch and placed it in the Doctor's hands.

Nova: "My dear friend, I am so sorry this happened to you. I promise you this: if there is a way in this universe to bring you back, I will. She is waiting for you, she needs you, I need you, and when you come back, then we will share this bottle together."

He went out of the car, looked at the distance, and saw Astra holding his brother by his shoulders, using both his hands and hitting him with his head. His brother's vitals dropped almost to zero. Nova ran, and with all his strength, tried to push Astra away from his brother. It was useless; it was like pushing a mountain. Then he remembered his training. He concentrated, and then the earth bellow Atra's feet began to shake. Suddenly, a big piece of row iron came out of the earth and hit Astra from below. He released One and fell on the ground, then that huge piece of iron flew to the sky and was left to drop on Astra's lying body. Astra opened his mouth and screamed like an animal being wounded. He was again bleeding, blood running from the edges of his grey uniform. Nova went where his brother was. He was badly hurt, and his half-naked body was covered in bruises and wounds.

One: "Don't let him win. That will be the end of my plan. That will be the end of me, of you."

Nova: "He is going to die here."

Nova raised his hand and the huge iron that was sitting on Astra's body started to melt. It became lava, it was so hot that it burned the atmosphere around it. Astra was still alive, and his uniform was still functioning; barely, though, but it was enough to protect him from the lava. Astra was alive, even after that. He managed slowly but steadily to stand up, his body resembling a cast-iron mould. He looked more like a statue than a living being. He ran and grabbed Nova's hands. Nova felt the heat and smelled his burning skin, Astra pulled him down to the ground and put his legs around his body. Nova was burning. He had no uniform to protect him, he only had his aura, which had created a shield around his skin, but that wasn't enough. The pain was unimaginable. He started losing conciseness, he knew he was near the end. He had no way of escaping this. Dr Stan was dead, his brother seriously injured, and he was burning. Moments before he lost his senses, moments before he died, a voice entered his mind, a known voice: it was his brother.

One: "You were always the stronger one, but you were always afraid of what you are. You hold back in fear of losing control like you did when we were infants. This is not a moment for you to hold back, this is the moment that you have to decide: do you live or die? I will give you the motivation you need. Look into my mind. I have no boundaries, the only thing you cannot see is my plan. The rest is there. Now look!"

Nova was inside One's mind, looking through his eyes. He was in her house, in Nickys house. She was sitting on the couch with her two kids. Dr Stan was there. That was the moment when he entered the room and took them, the moment he saved them. Then he saw himself entering the room, but how could his brother have seen him? How could he have any memories of that? He then witness the moment he touched his brother's head. He was looking through his brother's eyes and his brother was looking straight through his eyes. He saw him! He wasn't affected by the time freeze; he was aware of what happened. He wasn't tricked, he chose to let them all live. But why?

One: "I know where you have them and I promise you this: if you die here, I will leave this place, go and find them and kill them all. But before I do that, I will take her Dr Stan's head as a present. So now you have the choice: release your true powers and live, or die and they will die too."

Nova felt a void in him. Suddenly, every sound stopped. He stopped feeling pain, and something inside him was awaken. His eyes became black, his aura became black, his veins doubled their size. He looked at Astra, easily released his hands, and pushed him away using his legs. Astra was shocked - what was this transformation? This aura? He had fought all over existence, and he'd never encountered such an aura before. He was almost dead, how could he come up with such a power? How could he have transformed?

One was looking at the whole scene. He knew the outcome, it was obvious. Astra was no more. He walked towards Dr Stan's body, he got him naked, and took both his uniform and his helmet. Although the uniform was dead, it was still useful. It was necessary for his plan. That was what he needed form Dr Stan from the beginning, the helmet and the uniform, that was part of his plan, as well. He knew they would use him; he knew they would equip him. For some reason he felt sad, he wasn't expecting that the beaten-up body of Dr Stan would have any effect on him, but it did. It was the first time he had this feeling, he never before had any reason to experience it. He admired the Doctor and his devotion to his people. He respected him more after he saw him fight, and after he was in fact defeated by him. At this point, he decided that he could deviate a little from his plan. He had time for that. So, he took the Doctor's body with him and left the scene.

Meanwhile, Nova was yet fighting Astra, he was moving so fast that Astra couldn't even see him. Not even an experienced warrior like Astra could lock on his movements. Astra's body was at Nova's mercy, and believe me, he had no mercy to share. Punch after punch, kick after kick, Astra's body began to shut down. He couldn't even try to block the attacks anymore. All of his bones were broken to pieces. He was barely standing. His uniform gave up from the first two punches. He was bleeding from every possible place a human could bleed. It wasn't a fight anymore; it was a massacre. Moments before his heart stopped, Nova seized his attacks. Astra was now back to his normal form. Nova entered his mind, collected everything he could, then while already having his hands-on Astra's head, with one move, ripped his head off. He stayed like that for a moment; he was looking into Astra's eyes while the life faded out of him. He dropped his head next to his dead body, laid down on the ground, and closed his eyes. He knew his brother was already away, so no threat was near. What he didn't knew was that he took his friend's body with him.

One and the Doctor were already back at his cave. He was tired, he was hurting. This battle was far worse than the one he had with Dr Stan. He managed to recover from the first battle within a few hours, but he knew he couldn't do the same now. He needed more time. His internal organs were struggling to reproduce their vitals. He was so tired - actually, it was the first time in his life he felt tired. What a strange feeling, he thought, having your own body as a burden. He sat on the ground. He was practically naked as his clothes were destroyed previously. He saw the uniform lying next to him, and he put it on. The moment it touched his skin something happened to it; it changed to black; it was alive again. It seemed that his DNA somehow brought it back to life. He immediately took it off and put it on Dr Stan's dead body, then put the helmet on Doctor's head. The uniform was still black - it was working, but he couldn't feel any vital signs out of the Doctor's body. He mimicked the Doctor's previous movements and concentrated on collecting electricity. Slowly, between One's hands, a small ball of electricity came to be. He knew that too much of it would probably destroy both the uniform and the Doctor's body, so he stopped when he felt that the load was enough, then released it into his chest. The uniform on that area changed colour and went back to red, but within seconds, it was black again. The electric current had reached his heart. That was all that was needed, a small pulse, a tiny weak beat, the uniform did the rest. It pumped blood to his heart and started creating the necessary static in order to keep his whole system working. Blood was now running through his veins, oxygen was produced, and his temperature stately and slowly rose up. One was exhausted; that last trick he did took all of his remaining strength. He had shut down everything, he was a mere mortal now, but he had no choice. He needed to keep his vitals going until his body cured itself. He took a corner in the cave, put his back to the cave wall and closed his eyes. He was deeply sleeping, while a few metres away, the Doctor laid on the ground.

Nova was still in Nevada. There was something in the desert that offered him clarity, peace, understanding and the power to move on. On the one hand, he was holding the bottle he promised his friend that one day they would share, and on the other hand, another bottle, half-empty. He was reminiscing about his short actual life; from the day he was released out of that horrible tank of amniotic fluid up to this day. He missed his old life; the laboratory, the scientists, his tasks of solving mysteries and discovering new things for mankind, the four sponsors whose identities were known only to him, but most of all he missed his friend. He didn't even have his body to bury, his brother took it. But why? Why would he carry a dead body with him? Especially being as seriously wounded as he was. He knew there was a reason. His brother was a calculative machine, everything was part of an equation. He kept drinking until he fell asleep. He was in such a deep state of sleep that even if a plane crashed on him, he wouldn't feel it. He had a very strange dream: he was in a cave, his friend and his brother were there, and they were sitting at a big white table. They were both in black suits, and they were drinking champagne and laughing. They looked at him, they called him, so he went there and sat at the table. He took the glass of champagne his friend offered him. He couldn't understand what was going on, then his brother stood up, came next to him and offered him a toast. He refused and pushed his brother's hand away, then Dr Stan came there and looked Nova deep in the eyes.

Dr Stan: "The reason that you and me will meet again is your brother. Make the toast with him - this is the only way."

Nova: "The only way? For what?"

Dr Stan: "For everyone's survival."

Nova woke up. He was deep in sweat, and his heart was beating so fast he could feel it pushing his chest. This was not a dream, he thought. No, this was a message; he is alive! Somehow, he is alive, and he wanted Nova to find him. He made some coffee and tried to concentrate. He was trying to locate One's or Dr Stan's stigma, but it was impossible. The Doctor was still recovering and he was wearing the helmet, and One was practically a mere human.

Back in the cave, Dr Stan regained his consciousness and he was fully recovered. His memories had stopped at the moment of his death. The last thing he remembered was looking at Nova. Now he was in a cave, wearing his uniform and helmet. How did he get there? Who brought him? Then he sensed a very weak aura, so weak that it was almost untraceable. It was One; he was in the corner of the cave, naked and beaten up, his pulse low, his breathing heavy and slow. He was in a horrible state. The Doctor went to him. He wanted to know what happened, so he touched his head and entered his mind. He then saw everything that happened after he was attacked by Astra. He also saw his plan; so that was his plan. He saw everything, his whole life, the brutality his mind was exposed to, the one-sided history of mankind. He couldn't stand it anymore. He disengaged from him. He now knew he owed his life to him and he knew that he wasn't fooled into thinking he killed Nicky and the kids - he allowed them to live. He felt he owed him a lot - not only his own life, but hers, the kids', and Nova's. If he hadn't come, they would have been dead by now. He knew where to take him. He couldn't just take him to any hospital, he was the most wanted person on the whole planet - well, not actually wanted. A better and more appropriate word would be 'searched'. He was the most searched for person on the whole planet. He took him on his shoulders and started running. He could run faster than any human ever did. Actually, he could outrun all the existing animals on Earth. After approximately six hours of running, he stopped in front of a house, gently put One on the ground, and knocked the door. A woman opened the door. She was holding a glass of wine. She recognised him. He was different; his body had transformed, he looked taller, and although years had passed, he looked the same. She hugged him so tight that she dropped the glass of wine on the floor. He hugged her back.

Dr Lee: "They said you were dead…"

Dr Stan: "They said you were dead, too…"

Dr Lee: "What happened to you? You look different, you feel different. If I saw you from a distance, I could swear you were Nova."

Dr Stan: "It's a long story. Right now, we have more urgent things to do."

He went on the pavement, took One in his arms and brought him in the house. In the beginning, she couldn't recognise him; he looked much older, his naked body was covered in blood and bruises, and his white long hair was almost red from blood. One suddenly opened his eyes, and he looked around. His eyes stopped at Dr Lee. She recognized those eyes; she would recognize that red eye anywhere. She looked at Dr Stan, and he looked back at her. it was obvious what she was thinking, and she was right - that was the man who exterminated all of her colleagues, it was the man who nearly killed her. How could he now ask her to do this? He had no choice.

Dr Stan: "A lot has happened the last few days. I don't have the time to explain them to you right now, and I cannot touch your fragile mind. I need you to trust me - this man must live. You have the basic medical training; we need a place to stay and some treatment for him. Whatever happens, he cannot harm you. I am stronger than he is, I will protect you. I promise."

She then understood what was different with her old friend. He was somehow turned as one of them, but was he the same person? Her old friend would never bring him at her house and ask her to treat him. But what option did she actually have? If he was hostile then he would simply kill her if she refused. If he was indeed her friend, the same man she used to know, then she should trust him and do as he say. Her course of action was actually a one-way road. Before she even answered, Dr Stan looked at her, smiled, and thanked her. They put One on a couch. She brought her medical supplies, put him on a serum, treated his wounds, gave him painkillers, and made sure he was as conformable as possible.

Dr Stan: "Right now, at this moment, he is just a human. He is totally shut down. You could kill him with a kitchen knife if you wish."

Dr Lee: "I don't want to kill anyone. All I want is for you to explain to me what happened. And why the hell are you wearing that stupid thing on your head? You got bald or something?"

The two doctors laughed so hard that even One woke up. They looked at him and laughed even more. He then laughed as well and gave them the finger before he passed out.

Dr Stan: "I will tell you everything, but let me ask you something first. Do you have any single malts?"

Dr Lee: "No, I hate scotch. But I can order a bottle if you wish."

Dr Stan: "Nothing fancy, I drink almost anything that it is at least eighteen years old and single barrel. Oh, and please order me two bottles, just in case."

They sat there all night talking and drinking, and he hadn't told her everything. He just told her enough so she could generally understand what was going on. At some point, he decided to take his helmet off. He couldn't find a reason to keep it on his head. At that very moment, Nova spotted him. He never stopped looking, not even for a minute. After a couple of minutes, the doorbell wrang. Dr Stan smiled. He went and opened the door. It was his friend, holding a bottle of scotch.

Nova: "You don't remember this because you were a little

bit dead at the moment, but I promised you that this bottle would be shared between us."

Dr Stan: "No, I actually don't remember that, but I am happy that the specific bottle is here. Dr Lee has a terrible taste in alcohol."

Dr Lee: "Hey? Fuck off, both of you."

She stood up, went at the door and the three of them hugged and laughed. They were the sole survivors of their whole team. The strangest of things was the fact that the killer of their friends was on the couch with a serum and getting treated. Nova went inside and he saw his brother unconscious on the couch. He was in terrible shape; he hadn't expected him to be that bad. When he left the desert, he looked much better. Although they were brothers, they never spent time together, further than the period they were in their mother's womb, and later on that Russian military facility. But they had a strong bond together. He felt sad seeing him like that, although he was the absolute opposite of what he was, but at the end he was yet his twin brother. But after all, they had different backgrounds; his brother was raised to be the ultimate weapon, a man who could eliminate an army without even breaking a sweat. On the contrary, he was raised to be the epitome of capitalism, a machine creating money. He then wondered for the first time in his whole life if he would have been like his brother if he was in his place? Did his brother even have a chance? While he was thinking of all that, his brother opened his eyes. He saw Nova standing there, strong, proud, handsome, with his expensive blue suit. He smiled at him. He tried to stand up but he was yet too weak to do so. That electricity he had gathered in order to jumpstart Dr Stan's heart didn't come from the nature, he hadn't mastered that technique. That ball of energy came from his own body. This is why he was so overwhelmed; he had given almost everything he had. Nova felt bad for his brother. He sat next to him, put the blanket more up so it covered his whole body, touched his brother's forehead, and then went to the kitchen where the other two continued with their drinks.

Nova: "So... You are alive, ha? Not dead? Again? You made it a habit coming back from the dead."

He sat on the table, opened the bottle he kept for him and the Doctor, poured it into two glasses, gave one to the Doctor, and the other was already touching his lips.

Nova: "Dr Lee, nice to see you, too. I know what you've been through and I am sorry about everything."

Dr Lee: "Good to see you too, old friend. Now, shall we talk about the elephant in the room? Oh wait, it's not an elephant, and it is not in this room. It is a psychopathic murderer and he is in my living room."

Dr Stan: "First thing's first, cheers to you guys. Now I promise both of you that the third time I'll die will be the last one. Now, about the elephant - things changed. We have bigger concerns than him, and he is more than necessary for our survival, as we are for his. Let's call it a white marriage, shall we?"

While they were discussing, One got up, put on a pair of jumpsuits that were next to his couch, went into the bathroom, cleaned his face, and walked into the kitchen. His powers were off. He was yet a regular, red-eyed, white-haired, fully ripped man. As soon as he entered the room, everybody turned on him. They stopped talking, and they all wondered how could it be that this man, who minutes ago was in a situation between life and death, could be already standing and smiling.

One: "Dr Lee, I would like to thank you for your

hospitality and treatment. I can only imagine how difficult this must be for you, but if it makes you feel better, I would like you to know something. I felt your presence in the lab. I knew you were hiding in the amniotic tank, and I let you live. You are a very important and necessary person. You just don't know how important yet."

Dr Stan: "I don't believe you came here for a fight, correct?"

One: "Actually, I would like to have a glass of that scotch you are having. I have never tasted alcohol but I believe that there will never be a better time to do so."

Nova took a glass, looked at his brother, who in the meantime was already sitting across from him, and put some scotch in his glass. He poured him some out of that bottle that he saved for him and the Doctor."

Nova: "Why you are down?"

One: "I need the rest, brother, and there is no reason for it right now. It's a way of showing you I mean no harm. For now, at least, and if by any chance I was looking for trouble, I will find it from you. Your released powers are amazing. And by the way, I am really enjoying this verbal conversation. For some reason it makes better sense as it goes."

Dr Stan: "I saw your plan, you know this, don't you? I know what your goal is. From the one hand, I understand it; on the other, I don't. You don't fool me, you shut down your powers so you can lock your mind. Good move. I don't trust you; this I am telling you, but for some sadomasochist reason, I don't quite comprehend yet. You saved me and I saved you."

Nova: "My brother, my friend; it seems that out of the three of us, I am the one with the least knowledge of facts. But that may be better, as it is known that knowledge is a pain in the ass."

One: "Brother, what happened with Astra's body? I felt his death, so there must be a body or some remains of it."

Nova: "He is rotting in the Nevada dessert. He must be already half-eaten by wild animals. That is his contribution to our planet. He is being recycled."

One: "His helmet? The uniform?"

Nova: "Melted and destroyed. That technology is not needed here, although I can imagine why you would feel sad about it. Don't worry, we can handle ourselves without that. We will fight them together if they decide to interfere again, together as equals. Oh, and by saying so, Doctor, I believe we must destroy both your uniform and helmet. It is the only way in order to trust each other. No more secrets.

Before the Doctor had a chance to answer, a strange and intense smell was floating in the air. Both Nova and Dr Stan started feeling strangely dizzy. Nova recognized this; it was the same feeling he had when Dr Lee hypnotized him, but how it could this be? He was ready for that. His body create antibodies, he was supposed to be unaffected. Within moments, they both lost their consciousness. Dr Lee was there, petrified by fear. She didn't even move a muscle. One was standing now; you could feel that he was different, he had a heavier vibe. He was on. His powers were on.

One: "Don't be afraid, Doctor, I promise I will not hurt you or them. I just need a few things before I go. Oh, and when Nova wakes up, because he will wonder, tell him that all I did was to add another ingredient to your recipe. I just added some perfume, that was enough to fool his body. Great taste in perfumes, by the way, and thank you for keeping your stock here. You never know when it will be needed."

One took off Dr Stan's uniform and took his helmet as well, leaving him lying on the ground naked and unconscious. He then when to his brother, put his two hands around his head, stayed there for a couple of seconds, and then moved, heading to the front door.

One: "Doctor, one more time, I would like to thank you for everything, I can understand that you have questions. I have more. Please tell them that I have had a small change in my plans. I will make a little detour. When the time comes, they will understand. You see, evolution is adaptation, adaptation is adjusting, and of course, adjusting means changing. Things have changed - so have I.

He went out of the door and disappeared. Dr Lee tried to bring the two men back to their senses but it was useless. She searched for the antidote but One took it with him. She could do nothing more than just sit and wait until the effects of the hypnosis wore off. Seven hours passed, and the two men opened their eyes almost at the same time. The first thing they saw was two big cups of coffee waiting on the table. They looked at each other while reaching for their coffee, then they looked at Dr Lee, who was already coming their way from the living room. She was holding two bottles of painkillers. She gave them the pills, they opened the boxes, and without counting, took a hand-full of them and put them in their mouths while drinking their coffee.

Nova: "That went well. Dr Lee, would you be kind enough to keep us up to date? What happened and why I was hypnotised again by your stuff? And please tell me why he is only dressed with a blanket? I have a horrible headache and I cannot use my brain for anything more than just talking and hearing."

She told them everything that happened and everything One said. She explained to them that she was unable to wake them up sooner, and that most likely, because of lack of antidote, it would take some time for them to fully recover. They stayed there until they felt better, and when they did feel better and able to use their powers to one hundred per cent, they tried to located One; but as they already knew that was impossible. He was invisible to them now. He had the helmet, and he was stronger, he had the uniform. Dr Stan never told Nova about One's plan. He had his reasons. He buried it deep in his mind, it wasn't an accessible information. No matter how many times Nova tried to get him drunk, and despite the fact that a lot of times, Nova did get him wasted, that remained a secret. But it didn't actually matter anymore. The original plan was changed. One was nowhere to be found and life went on. Days passed, months, years. Some things changed, some remained, some didn't even matter anymore.

Three years had come to pass, and the G.O.D project was no more - but the government was still interested in Nova, and Dr Stan, of course. A special unit was created at the Pentagon, in memory of all who had died in the past. They kept the code, the acronyms, they kept G.O.D, but it was not labelled as a project anymore - it was G.O.D's division. Dr Stan got the same contract and benefits Nova had in the first place. He was now living with Nicky and her kids. He was now aware that you cannot protect the people you love from everything; you can, though, offer them as much as you can, and make sure they feel your love and care, for as long as it lasts. Nova was enjoying the benefits of a single man's life. He was the biggest economic burden of the whole division, and he was a common subject of discussion whenever a complimentary budget was asked. He was worth it, though. This time they didn't work for big interests and breakthroughs; this time they were mainly being used for espionage and advice. Also, the division had a black ops squadron, but Nova and Dr Stan made it clear they wanted nothing to do with that. Nova was continuously trying to communicate with his brother, to locate him. He was both worried about him, and for him. They never told anyone about Astra, and they didn't share the information they had about the others, or about the humankind origins. They knew that this would create tensions, unnecessary preparations and reactions from humanity; and also, if it somehow reached the public, riots would rise, a religious breakdown, and everything that would come with it. Nova hasn't really changed. Years have passed, but in his essence, he is the same man that came out of that tank. He knows more, he's been places, done things, but at the end, he is as the beginning. Dr Lee is now living outside of the USA. She is in Rome with her wife, and she teaches in a small local university, she is happy with everything her simple life has to offer. She tried to forget her previous employment and employers. Our story ends with Nova in his luxurious penthouse, looking up at the night sky, and wondering, wondering if his brother is alive, if the others will come to take revenge for Astra, and if they even know about Astra's interference. Then he opens his favourite single malt, lights up a cigar and sits on his leather couch. He sees one more time the night sky, takes a sip of scotch, and smiles…